THE MAKESHIFT ROCKET

A low murmur filled the cabin as the rearmost beer barrel snorted its vapours into space. There was a faint backward tug of acceleration pressure, which mounted very gradually as mass decreased. The thrust was not centred with absolute precision, and of course the distribution of mass throughout the whole structure was hit-or-miss, so the boat began to pick up a spin again. Steering by the seat of his pants and a few primitive meters, Herr Syrup corrected that tendency with side jets.

Blowing white beer fumes in all directions, the messenger boat moved slowly along a wobbling spiral . . .

THE
MAKESHIFT
ROCKET

POUL ANDERSON

Hamlyn Paperbacks

THE MAKESHIFT ROCKET

ISBN 0 600 37609 5

First published in Great Britain 1969
by Dobson Books Ltd.
Hamlyn Paperbacks edition 1978
Copyright © 1962 by Ace Books, Inc.
Magazine serial version, copyright, 1958
by Street and Smith Publications Inc.

Hamlyn Paperbacks are published by
The Hamlyn Publishing Group Ltd,
Astronaut House,
Feltham,
Middlesex, England

Made and printed in Great Britain
by Hazell Watson & Viney Ltd, Aylesbury, Bucks

CHAPTER ONE

'*Mercury Girl*, Black Sphere Line of Anguklukkakok City, Venusian Imperium, requesting permission to land and discharge cargo.'

'Ah. Yes,' said the large red haired man in the visiscreen. 'Venusian ownership, eh? An' what might your registry be?' Captain Dhan Gopal Radhakrishnan blinked mild brown eyes in some astonishment and said: 'Panamanian, of course.'

'Was that your last port of call?'

'No, we came via Venus. But I say, what has this to do with—'

'Let me see, let me see.' The man in the screen rubbed a gigantic paw across a freckled snub nose. He was young and cheerful of appearance; but since when had the portmaster of Grendel – of any asteroid in the Anglian Cluster – worn a uniform of such blazing green?

'An' might I hear what cargo ye have consigned locally?' he asked. It was definitely not a Grendelian accent he had. York? Scotia? No. Possibly New Belfast. Having maintained his Earthside home for years in Victoria, B.C., Captain Radhakrishnan fancied himself a student of English dialects. However—

'A thousand cases of Nashornbräu Beer and six ten-ton barrels of same, miscellaneous boxes of pretzels and popcorn, all for the Alt Heidelberg Rathskeller,' he answered. 'Plus goods for other ports, of course, notably a shipment of exogenetic cattle embryos for Alamo. Those have all been cleared for passage through intermediate territories.'

'Indeed. Indeed.' The young man nodded with a sharpness that bespoke decision. ' 'Tis all right, then. Give us a location signal an' folly the GCA beam in to Berth Ten.'

Captain Radhakrishnan acknowledged and signed off, adjusting his monocle nervously the while. Something was not all right. Definitely not. He turned the console over to the mate and switched the ship's intercom to *Engine Room*. 'Bridge speaking,' he intoned. 'I say, Mr. Syrup, have you any notion what's going on here?'

Knud Axel Syrup, chief and only engineer of the *Mercury Girl*, started and looked over his shoulder. He had been cheating at solitaire. 'Not'ing, skipper, yust not'ing,' he mumbled, tucking a beer bottle under a heap of cotton waste. His pet crow Claus leered cynically from a perch on a fuel line, but for a wonder remained silent.

'You weren't tuned in to my talk with the portmaster chap?'

Herr Syrup rose indignantly to his feet. He even sucked in his paunch. 'I ban tending to my own yob,' he said. 'Ban busier dan a Martian in rutting season. Ven are de owners going to install a new Number Four spinor? Every vatch I got to repair ours vit' chewing gum and baling vire.'

'When this old bucket of rust earns enough to justify it,' sighed Radhakrishnan's voice. 'You know as well as I do, she's barely paying her own way. But what I meant to say is, this portmaster chap. Got a brogue you could put soles on, y'know, and wearing some kind of uniform I never saw before.'

'Hm.' Herr Syrup rubbed his shining bald pate and scratched the fringe of brownish hair beneath it. He blew out his blond walrus mustache, blinked watery blue eyes, and ventured: 'Maybe he is from de Erse Cluster. I don't t'ink you ever ban dere; I vas vunce. It's approaching conyunction vit' Anglia now. Maybe he come here and got a yob.'

'But his uniform—'

'So dey changed de uniform again. Who can keep track of all dese little nations in de Belt, ha?'

'Mmmm – well, perhaps. Perhaps. Though I wonder – something dashed odd, don't y' know— Well, no matter, as you say, no matter, no matter. Got to carry on. Stand by for approach and landing, maneuver to commence in ten minutes.'

'*Ja, ja, ja,*' grumbled Herr Syrup. He fetched out his bottle, finished it, and tossed it into the waste chute which sponged it into space. Before he rang for his deckhand assistant, Mr Shubbish, he put a blue jacket over his tee shirt and an officer's cap on his head. The uniform was as faded and weary as the ship; more so, perhaps, for he made an effort to keep the vessel patched, painted, and scrubbed.

A long blunt-nosed cylinder, meteor-pocked, patchplated and rust-streaked from many atmospheres, the *Mercury Girl* departed freefall orbit and spiraled toward the asteroid. The first thing she lost was an impressive collection of beer bottle satellites. Next she lost her crew's temper, for the aged compensator developed a sudden flutter under deceleration and the men and Martians found their internal gyrogravitic field varying sinusoidally between 0.5 and 1.7 Earth gees.

That was uncomfortable enough to make them forget the actual hazard it added. Landing on a terraformed worldlet is tricky enough under the best conditions. The gyrogravitic generators at its center of mass are not able to increase the potential energy of the entire universe, but must content

3

themselves with holding a reasonable atmospheric envelope. Accordingly, their field is so heterodyned that the force is an almost level one gee for some 2000 kilometers up from the surface; then, within the space of a single kilometer, the artificial attraction drops to zero and the acceleration experienced is merely that due to the asteroid's mass. Crossing such a boundary is no simple task. It is made worse by the further heterodyning as the spaceship's negative force interacts with the terraformer's positive pull. When the crew are, in addition, plagued with unexpected rhythmic variations in their weight, a smooth transition becomes downright impossible.

Thus the *Mercury Girl* soared to boundary altitude, yawed, spun clear around, bounced a few times, and bucketed her way groundward, shuddering. She scraped steel as she entered berth, with a screech that set teeth on edge at Grendel's antipodes, rocked, came to a halt, and slowly stopped, groaning.

'*Fanden i helvede!*' roared Herr Syrup at the intercom. 'Vat kind of a landing do you call dat? I svear de beer is so shook up it explodes! By yumping Yudas—'

'*Sacre bleu!*' added Claus, fluttering about on ragged black wings. '*Teufelschwantzen und Schwefel!* Damn, blast, fap!'

'Now, now, Mr. Syrup,' said Captain Radharkrishnan soothingly. 'Now, now, now. After all, my dear fellow, I don't wish to make, ah, invidious comparisons, but the behavior of the internal field was scarcely what – what I could expect? Yes. What I would expect. In fact, the cook has just reported himself ill with, ah, what I believe is the first case of seasickness recorded in astronautical history.'

Herr Syrup, who had dropped and broken a favorite pipe, was in no mood to accept criticism. He barked an order to Mr. Shubbish, to rip the guts out of the compensator in lieu of its manufacturer, and stormed up the companionway and along clangorous passages to the bridge, where he pushed open the door so it crashed and blew in like a profane whirlwind.

'My dear old chap!' exclaimed the captain. 'I say! Please! What will they think?'

'Vat vill obscenity who blankety-blank t'ink?'

'The portmaster and, ah, the other gentleman – there.' Radhakrishnan pointed at the main viewport and made agitated adjustments to his turban and jacket. 'Most irregular. I don't understand it. But he insisted we remain inboard until— Dear, dear, *do* you think you could get some of the tarnish off this braid of mine before—'

Knud Axel Syrup stared at the outside view. Beyond the little spacefield was a charming vista of green meadows, orderly hedgerows, cottages and bowers, a white gravel road. Just below the near, sharply curving horizon stood Grendel's only town; from this height could be seen a few roofs and the twin spires of St. George's. The flag of the Kingdom, a Union Jack on a Royal Stuart field, fluttered there under a sky of darker blue than Earth's, a small remote sun and a few of the brightest stars. Grendel was a typical right little, tight little Anglian asteroid, peacefully readying for the vacation-season influx of tourists from Briarton, York, Scotia, Holm, New Winchester, and the other shires.

Or was it? For the flagstaff over the spaceport carried an alien banner, white, with a shamrock and harp in green. The two men striding over the concrete toward the ship wore clover-colored tunics and trousers, military boots and sidearms. Similarly uniformed men paced along the wire fence or waited by machine gun nests. Not far away was berthed a space freighter, almost as old and battered as the *Girl* but considerably larger. And – and—

'*Pest og forbandelse!*' exclaimed Herr Syrup.

'What?' Captain Radhakrishnan swiveled worried eyes toward him.

'Plague and damnation,' translated the engineer courteously.

'Eh? Where?'

'Over dere.' Herr Syrup pointed. 'Dat odder ship. Don't you see? Dere is a gun turret coupled onto her!'

'Well – I'll be – goodness gracious,' murmured the captain.

Steps clanging on metal and a hearty roar drifted up to the bridge, together with a whiff of cool country air. In a few moments the large redhead entered the bridge. Behind him trailed a very tall, very thin, and very grim-looking middle-aged man.

'The top of the mornin' to yez,' boomed the young one. He attempted a salute. 'Major Rory McConnell of the Shamrock League Irredentist Expeditionary Force, *at* your ser-r-r-vice!'

'What?' exclaimed Radharkrishnan. He gaped and lifted his hands. 'I mean – I mean to say, don't y' know, what? Has a war broken out? Or has it? Mean to say, y' know,' he babbled, 'we've had no such information, but then we've been en route for some weeks and—'

'Well, no.' Major Rory McConnell shoved back his disreputable cap with a faint air of embarrassment. 'No, your honor, 'tis not exactly a war we're havin'. More an act of justice.'

The thin, razor-creased man shoved his long nose forward. 'Perhaps I should explain,' he clipped, 'bein' as I am in command here. 'Tis indeed an act of necessary an' righteous justice we are performin', after what the spalpeens did to us forty years agone come St. Matthew's Day.' His dark eyes glowed fanatically. 'The fact is, in order to assert the rightful claims of the Erse nation ag'inst the unprovoked an' shame-

6

less aggression of the – pardon me language – English of the Anglian Kingdom. The fact is, this asteroid is now under military occupation.' He clicked his heels and bowed. 'Permit me to introduce meself. General Scourge of the Sassenach O'Toole, of the Shamrock League Irredentist—'

'*Ja, ja,*' said Herr Syrup. He still carried a cargo of anger to unload on someone. 'I heard all dat. I also heard dat de Shamrock League is only a political party in de Erse Cluster.'

Scourge-of-the-Sassenach O'Toole winced. 'Please, *Saorstat Erseann.*'

'So vat you ban doin' vit' a private filibustering expedition, ha? And vat has it got to do vit' us?'

'Well,' said Major Rory McConnell, not quite at ease, 'the fact is, your honors, I'm sorry to be sayin' it, but ye can't leave here just the now.'

'What?' cried Captain Radhakrishnan. 'Can't leave? What do you mean, sir?' He drew himself up to his full 1.6 meters. 'This is a Venusian ship, may I remind you, of Terrestrial registry, and engaged on its – er, ahem – its lawful occasions. Yes, that's it, its lawful occasions. You can't detain us!'

McConnell slapped his sidearm with a meaty hand. 'Can't we?' he asked, brightening.

'But – look here – see here, my dear chap, we're on schedule. We're expected at Alamo, don't y' know, and if we don't report in—'

'Yes. There is that. 'Tis been anticipated.' General O'Toole squinted at them. Suddenly he pointed a bony finger at the engineer. 'Yez! What might your name be?'

'I ban Knud Axel Syrup of Simmerboelle, Langeland,' said the engineer indignantly, 'and I am going to get in touch vit' de Danish consul at—'

'Mister *who*?' interrupted McConnell.

'Syrup!' It is a perfectly good Danish name, though like Middlefart it is liable to misinterpretation by foreigners. 'I vill call my consulate on New Vinshester, *ja*, by Yudas, I vill even call de vun on Tara in Erse—'

'*Teamhair*,' corrected O'Toole, wincing again.

'You see,' said Radhakrishnan, anxiously fingering his monocle, 'our cargo to Alamo carries a stiff penalty clause, and if we're held up here any length of time, then—'

'Quiet!' barked O'Toole. His finger stabbed toward the Earthmen. 'So 'twas Venus ye were on last, eh? Well, as military commandant of this occupied asteroid, I hereby appoints meself medical officer an' I suspect ye of carryin' Polka Dot Plague.'

'Polka Dot!' bellowed Herr Syrup. A red flush went up from his hairy chest till his scalp gleamed like a landing light. 'Vy, you spoutnosed son of a Svedish politician, dere hasn't been a case of Polka Dot in all de Imperium for twenty-five Eart' years!'

'Possibly,' snapped O'Toole. 'However, under international law the medical officer of any port has a right an' duty to hold any vessel in quarantine whin he suspects a dangerous disease aboard. I suspects of Polka Dot Plague, an' this whole asteroid is hereby officially quarantined.'

'But!' wailed Radhakrishnan.

'I think six weeks will be long enough,' said O'Toole more gently. 'Meanwhile ye'll be free to move about an'—'

'Six weeks here will ruin us!'

'Sorry, sir,' answered McConnell. He beamed. 'But take heart, ye're bein' ruined in a good cause: redressin' the wrongs of the Gaelic race!'

CHAPTER TWO

Fuming away on a pipe which would have been banned under any smog-control ordinance, Knud Axel Syrup bicycled into Grendel Town. He ignored the charm of thatch and tile roofs, half-timbered Tudor facades, and swinging signboards. Those were for tourists, anyway; Grendel lived mostly off the vacation trade. But it did not escape him how quiet the place was, its usual cheerful pre-season bustle dwindled to a tight-lipped housewife at the greengrocer's and a bitterly silent dart game in the Crown & Castle.

Occasionally a party of armed Erse, or a truck bearing the shamrock sign, went down the street. The occupying force seemed composed largely of very young men, and it was not professional. The uniforms were homemade, the arms a wild assortment from grouse guns up through stolen rocket launchers, the officers were saluted when a man happened to feel like saluting, and the idea that it might be a nice gesture to march in step had never occurred to anyone.

Nevertheless, there were something like a thousand invaders on Grendel, and their noisy, grinning, well-meaning sloppiness did not hide the fact that they could be tough to fight.

Herr Syrup stopped at the official bulletin board in the market square. Brushing aside ivy leaves, the announcement of a garden party at the vicarage three months ago, and a yellowing placard wherein the Lord Mayor of Grendel invited bids for the construction of a fen country near the

Heorot Hills, he found the notice he was looking for. It was gaudily hand-lettered in blue and green poster paints and said:

Know all men by these presents, that forty Earth-years ago, when the planetoid clusters of Saorstat Erseann and the Anglian Kingdom were last approaching conjunction, the asteroid called Lois by the Anglians but rightfully known to its Erse discoverer Michael Boyne as Laoighise (pronounced Lois) chanced to drift between the two nations on its own skewed orbit. An Anglian prospecting expedition landed, discovered rich beds of praseodymium, and claimed the asteroid in the name of King James IV. The Erse Republic protested this illegal seizure and sent a warship to remove the Anglian squatters, only to find that King James IV had caused two warships to be sent; accordingly, despite this severe provocation, the peace-loving Erse Republic withdrew its vessel. The aforesaid squatters installed a powerful gyrogravitic unit on Laoighise and diverted its orbit into union with the other planetoids of the Anglian Cluster. Since then Anglia has remained in occupation and exploitation.

The Erse Republic has formally protested to the World Court, on the clear grounds that Michael Boyne, an Erse citizen, was the first man to land on this body. The feeble Anglian argument that Boyne did not actually claim it for his nation and made no effort to ascertain its possible value, cannot be admissible to any right-thinking man; but for forty Earth-years the World Court, obviously corrupted by Stuart gold, has upheld this specious contention.

Now that the Erse and Anglian nations are again orbiting close toward each other, the Shamrock League Irredentist Expeditionary Force has set about rectifying the situation. This is a patriotic organization which, though it does not have the backing of its own government at the moment, expects that this approval will be forthcoming and retroactive as soon as our sacred mission has succeeded. Therefore, the Shamrock League Irredentist Expeditionary Force is not piratical, but operating under international laws of war, and the Geneva Convention applies. As a first step in the recovery of Laoighise, the Shamrock League Irredentist Expeditionary Force finds it necessary to occupy the asteroid Grendel.

All citizens are therefore enjoined to cooperate with the occupying authorities. The personnel and property rights of civilians will be respected provided they refrain from interference with the lawfully constituted authorities, namely ourselves. All arms and communications equipment must be surrendered for sequestration. Any attempt to leave Grendel or communicate beyond its atmosphere is forbidden and punishable under the rules of war. All citizens are reminded again that the Shamrock League Irredentist Expeditionary Force is here for a legitimate purpose which is to be respected.

Erin go bragh!
General Scourge-of-the-Sassenach O'Toole
Commanding Officer, S.L.I.E.F.
per: Sgt. 1/cl Daniel O'Flaherty
(New Connaught O'Flahertys)

'Ah,' said Herr Syrup. 'So.'
He pedaled glumly on his way. These people seemed to mean business.

Though he sometimes lost his temper, Knud Axel Syrup was not a violent man. He had seen his share of broken knuckles, from St. Pauli to Hellport to Jove Dock; he much preferred a mug of beer and a friendly round of pinochle. The harbor girls could expect no more from him than a fatherly smile and a not quite fatherly pat; he had his Inga back in Simmerboelle. She was a good wife, aside from her curious idea that he would instantly fall a prey to pneumonia without an itchy scarf around his neck. Her disapproval of the myriad little nations which had sprung up throughout the Solar System since gyrogravitics made terraforming possible was more vocal than his; but, in a mild and tolerant way, he shared it. Home's best.

Nevertheless, a man had some right to be angry! For instance, when a peso-pinching flock of Venusian owners, undoubtedly with more scales on their hearts than even their backs, made him struggle along with a spinor that should have been scrapped five years ago. But what, he asked himself, is a man to do? There were few berths available for the aging crew of an aging ship, without experience in the latest and sleekest apparatus. If the *Mercury Girl* went on the beach, so, most likely, did Knud Axel Syrup. Of course, there would be a nice social worker knocking at his home to offer a nice Earthside job – say, the one who had already mentioned a third assistantship in a food-yeast factory – and Inga would make sure he wore his nice scarf every day. Herr Syrup shuddered and pushed his bicycle harder.

At the end of Flodden Field Street he found the tavern he was looking for. Grendel did not try exclusively for an Old Tea Shoppe atmosphere. The Alt Heidelberg Rathskeller stood between the Osmanli Pilaff and Pizen Pete's Last Chance Saloon. Herr Syrup leaned his bicycle against the wall and pushed through an oak door carved with the image of legendary Gambrinus.

The room downstairs was appropriately long, low, and smoky-raftered. Rough-hewn tables and benches filled a candle-lit gloom; great beer barrels lined the walls; sabers hung crossed above rows of steins which informed the world that *Gutes Bier und junge Weiber sind die besten Zeitvertreiber*. But it was empty. Even for midafternoon, there was something ominous about the silence. The Stuart legitimists who settled the Anglian Cluster had never adopted the closing laws of the mother country.

Herr Syrup planted his stocky legs and stared around. 'Hallo!' he called. 'Hallo, dere! Is you home, Herr Bachmann?'

It slithered in the darkness behind the counter. A Martian came out. He stood fairly tall for a Martian, his hairless gray cupola of a head-cum-torso reaching past the Earthman's waist, and his four thick walking tentacles carried him across the floor with a speed unusual for his race in Terrestrial gravity. His two arm-tentacles writhed incoherently, his flat nose twitched under the immense brow, his wide lipless mouth made bubbling sounds, his bulging eyes rolled in distress of soul. As he came near, Herr Syrup saw that he had somehow poured himself into an embroidered blouse and *lederhosen*. A Tyrolean hat perched precariously on top of him.

'*Ach!*' he piped. 'Wer da? Wilkommen, mein dear friend, sitzen here and—'

'*Gud bevare's,*' said the engineer, catching his pipe as it fell from his jaws, 'vat's going on here? Vere is old Hans Bachmann?'

'Ach, he has retired,' said the Martian. 'I have taken over der business. Pardon me, I mean I have der business overgetaken.' He stopped in front of his guest, extending three boneless fingers. 'My name is Sarmishkidu. I mean, Sarmishkidu von Himmelschmidt. Sit down make yourself *gemütlich.*'

'Vell, I am Knud Axel Syrup of de *Mercury Girl*.'

'Ah, the ship what is bringing me mine beer? Or was? Well, have a drink.' The Martian scuttled off, drew two steinsful, came back and writhed himself onto the bench across the table at which the Earthman had sat down. '*Prosit*.'

A Martian standing anyone a beer was about the most astonishing event of this day. But it was plain to see that Sarmishkidu von Himmelschmidt was not himself. His skin twitched as he filled a Tyrolean pipe, and he fanned himself with his elephantine ears.

'How did you happen to enter dis business?' asked Herr Syrup, trying to put him more at ease.

'Ach! I came here last Uttu-year – Mars-year – on sabbatical. I am a professor of mathematics at Enliluraluma University.' Since every citizen of Enliluraluma has some kind of position at the University, usually in the math department, Herr Syrup was not much impressed. 'At that time this enterprise was most lucrative. Extrapolating probabilistically, I induced myself to accept Herr Bachmann's offer of a transfer of title. I invested all my own savings and obtained a mortgage on Uttu for the balance—'

'Oh, oh,' said Herr Syrup, sympathetically, for not even the owners of the Black Sphere Line could be as ruthless as any and all Martian bankers. They positively enjoyed foreclosing. They made a ceremony of it, at which dancing clerks strewed cancelled checks while a chorus of vice presidents sang a litany. 'And now business is not so good, vat?'

'Business is virtually at asymptotic zero,' mourned Sarmishkidu. 'The occupation, you know. We are cut off from the rest of the universe. And vacation season coming in two weeks! The Erse do not plan to leave for six weeks yet, at a minimum – and meanwhile this entire planetoid will have been diverted into a new orbit off the regular trade lanes – possibly ruined in the fighting around Lois. In view of all this uncertainty, even local trade has slacked off to negligibility. *Ach, es ist ganz schrecklich!* I am ruined!'

'But if I remember right,' said Herr Syrup, bewildered, 'New Vinshester, de Anglian capital, is only about ten t'ousand kilometers from here. Vy do dey not send a varship?'

'They are not aware of it,' said Sarmishkidu, burying his flat face in the tankard. 'Excuse me, I mean they do not know what fumblydiddles is here going on. Before vacation time, we never get many ships here. Der Erses landed just four days ago. They took ofer *der Rundfunk*, the radio, and handled routine messages as if nothing had happened. Your ship was the first since der invasion.'

'And may be de last,' groaned Herr Syrup. 'Dey made some qvack-qvack about plague and qvarantined us.'

'Ach, so!' Sarmishkidu passed a dramatic hand over his eyeballs. 'Den ve iss ruined for certain. Dot iss just the excuse the Erses have been wanting. Now they can call New Winchester, making like they was der real medical officer, and say the whole place is quarantined on suspicion of plague. So natural, no one else vill land for six weeks, so they not be quarantined too and maybe even get sick. Your owners is also notified and does not try to investigate what has happened. So for six weeks the Erses has a free hand here to do what they want. Und what they want to do means the ruin of all Grendel!'

'My captain is still arguing vit' de Erse general,' said Herr Syrup. 'I am yust de engineer. But I come down to see if I could save us anyt'ing. Even if ve lose money because of not delivering our cargo to Alamo, maybe at least ve get paid for de beer ve bring you. No?'

'*Gott in Himmel!* Without vacation season business like I

was counting on, where vould I find the moneys to pay you?'

'I vas afraid of dat,' said Herr Syrup.

He sat drinking and smoking and trying to persuade himself that an Earthside job as assistant in a yeast factory wasn't really so bad. Himself told him what a liar he was.

The door opened, letting in a shaft of sun, and light quick steps were heard. A feminine voice cried: 'Rejoice!'

Herr Syrup rose clumsily. The girl coming down the stairs was worth rising for, being young and slim, with a shining helmet of golden hair, large blue eyes, pert nose, long legs, and other well-formed accessories. Her looks were done no harm by the fact that – while she avoided cosmetics – she wore a short white tunic, sandals, a laurel wreath on her head, and nothing else.

'Rejoice!' she cried again, and burst into tears.

'Now, now,' said Herr Syrup anxiously. 'Now, now, *Froeken* . . . er, Miss – now, now, now, yust a minute.'

The Martian had already gone over to her. 'That is *nicht* so bad, Emily,' he whistled, standing on tiptentacle to pat her shoulder. 'There, there. Remember Epicurus.'

'I don't care about Epicurus!' sobbed the girl, burying her face in her hands.

'*Outis epoisei soi bareias cheiras,*' said Sarmishkidu bravely.

'Well,' wept the girl, 'w-well, of course. At least, I hope so.' She dabbed at her eyes with a laurel leaf. 'I'm sorry. It's just that – that – oh, everything.'

'Yes,' said the Martian, 'the situation indubitably falls within the Aristotelian definition of tragedy. I have calculated my losses so far at a net fifty pounds sterling, four shillings and thruppence ha'penny per diem.'

Wet, but beautiful, the girl blinked at Herr Syrup. 'Pardon me, sir,' she said tremulously. 'This situation on Grendel, you know. It's so overwreaking.' She put her finger to her lips and frowned. 'Is that the word? These barbarian languages! I mean, the situation has us all overwrought.'

'Ahem!' said Sarmishkidu. 'Miss Emily Croft, may I present Mister, er—'

'Syrup,' said Herr Syrup, and extended a somewhat engine-grimy hand.

'Rejoice,' said the girl politely. '*Hellenicheis?*'

'Gesundheit,' said Herr Syrup.

Miss Emily Croft stared, then sighed. 'I asked if you spoke Attic Greek,' she said.

'No, I'm sorry, I do not even speak basement Greek,' floundered Herr Syrup.

'You see,' said Miss Croft, 'I am a Duncanite – even if it does make Father furious. He's the vicar, you know – and I'm the only Duncanite on Grendel. Mr. Sarmishkidu – I'm sorry, I mean Herr von Himmelschmidt – speaks Greek with me, which does help, even though I cannot always approve his choice of passages for quotation.' She blushed.

'Since ven has a Martian been talking Greek?' asked the engineer, trying to get some toehold on reality.

'I found a knowledge of the Greek alphabet essential to my study of Terrestrial mathematical treatises,' explained Sarmishkidu, 'and having gone so far, I proceeded to learn the vocabulary and grammar as well. After all, time is money, I estimate my time as being conservatively worth five pounds an hour, and so by using knowledge already acquired for one purpose as the first step in gaining knowledge of another field, I saved study time worth almost—'

'But I'm afraid Herr von Himmelschmidt is not a follower of the doctrines of the Neo-Classical Enlightenment,' interrupted Emily Croft. 'I mean, as first expounded by Isadora and Raymond Duncan. I regret to say that Herr von Himmelschmidt is only interested in the, er,' she blushed again, charmingly, 'less laudable passages out of Aristophanes.'

'They are *filthy*,' murmured Sarmishkidu with a reminiscent leer.

'And I mean, please don't think I have any race prejudices or anything,' went on the girl, 'but it's just undeniable that Herr von Himmelschmidt isn't, well, isn't meant for classical dancing.'

'No,' agreed Herr Syrup after a careful study. 'No, he is not.'

Emily cocked her head at him. 'I don't suppose you would be interested?' Her tone was wistful.

Herr Syrup rubbed his bald pate, blew out his drooping mustache, and looked down past his paunch at his Number Twelve boots. 'Is classical dancing done barefoot?' he asked.

'Yes! And vine crowned, in the dew at dawn!'

'I vas afraid of dat,' sighed Herr Syrup. 'No, t'anks.'

'Well,' said the girl. Her head bent a little.

'But I am not so bad at de hambo,' offered Herr Syrup.

'No, thank you,' said Miss Croft.

'Vill you not sit down and have a beer vit' us?'

'Zeus, no!' She grimaced. 'How could you? I mean, that awful stuff just calcifies the liver.'

'Miss Croft drinken only der pure spring vater und eaten der fruits,' said Sarmishkidu von Himmelschmidt rather grimly.

'Well, but really, Mister Syrup,' said the girl, 'it's ever so much more natural than, oh, all this raw meat and – well, I mean if we had no other reason to know it, couldn't you just tell the Erse are barbarians from that dreadful stuff they drink, and all the bacon and floury potatoes and – Well, I mean to say, really.'

Herr Syrup sat down by his stein, unconvinced. Emily

perched herself on the table top and accepted a few grapes from a bowl of same which Sarmishkidu handed her in a gingerly fashion. The Martian then scuttled back to his own beer and pipe and a dish of pretzels.

'Do you know yust vat dese crazy Ersers is intending to do, anyhow?' asked Herr Syrup.

The girl clouded up again. 'That's what I came to see you about, Mr. Sarmishkidu,' she said. Her pleasant lower lip quivered. 'That terrible Major McConnell! The big noisy red one. I mean, he keeps speaking to me!'

'I am afraid,' began the Martian, 'that it is not in my province to—'

'Oh, but I mean, he stopped me in the street just now! He, he bowed and – and asked me to – Oh, no!' Emily buried her face in her hands trembling.

'To vat?' barked Herr Syrup, full of chivalrous indignation.

'He asked me if . . . if . . . I would . . . oh . . . would *go to the cinema* with him!'

'Vy, vat is playing?' asked Herr Syrup, interested.

'How should I know? It certainly isn't Aeschylus. It isn't even Euripides!' Emily raised a flushed small countenance and shifted gears to wrath. 'I thought, Mr Sarmishkidu, I mean, we've been friends for a while now and we Greeks have to stick together and all that sort of thing, couldn't you just refuse to sell him whisky? I mean, it would teach those barbarians a lesson, and it might even make them go home again, if they couldn't buy whisky, and Major McConnell wouldn't get a calcified liver.'

'Speak of the divvil!' bawled a hearty voice. Huge, military boots crashed on the stairs and Major Rory McConnell, all 200 redhaired centimeters of him, stalked down into the rathskeller. 'Pour me a drop of cheer, boy. No, set out the bottle an' we'll figure the score whin I'm done. For 'tis happy this day has become!'

'Don't!' blazed Emily, leaping to her feet.

'*Aber, aber* that whisky I sell at four bob the shot,' said Sarmishkidu, slithering hastily off his bench.

Major McConnell made a gallant flourish toward the girl. 'To be sure,' he roared, 'there's no such thing as an unhappy day wi' this colleen about. Surely the good God was in a rare mood whin she was borned, perhaps His favorite littlest angel had just won the spellin' prize, for faith an' I nivver seen a sweeter bundle of charms, not even on the Auld Sod herself whin I made me pilgrimage.'

'Do you see what happens to people who, who eat meat and drink distilled beverages?' said Emily to Herr Syrup. 'They just turn into absolute oafs. I mean to say, you can hear their great feet stamping two kilometers off.'

McConnell sprawled onto a bench, leaning against the table and resting his great feet on the floor at the end of prodigious legs. He winked at the Earthman. 'She's the light darlin' on her toes,' he agreed, 'but then she's not just overburdened wi' clothing. Whin I make her me missus, that'll have to be changed a bit, but for now 'tis pleasant the sight is.'

'Your wife?' screamed Emily. 'Why – why—' She fought valiantly with herself. At last, in a prim tone: 'I won't say anything, Major McConnell, but you will find my reply in Aristophanes, *The Frogs*, lines—'

'Here the bottle is,' said Sarmishkidu, returning with a flask labelled *Callahan's Rose of Tralee* 125 *Proof*. 'Und mind you,' he added, rolling a suspicious doorknob eye at the Erseman, 'when it comes to paying the score, we will make with the analytical balances to show how much you have *getaken*.'

'So be it.' McConnell yanked out the stopper and raised the bottle. 'To the Glory of God an' the Honor of Ireland!' He caught Herr Syrup's eye and added politely: '*Skaal.*'

The Dane lifted a grudging stein to him.

' 'Tis the find day for celebratin',' burbled McConnell. 'I've had the word from the engineering corps; our new droive unit tests out one hundred percent. They'll have it ready to go in three weeks.'

'Oh!' gasped Emily. She retreated into a dark corner behind a beer keg. Even Sarmishkidu began to look seriously worried.

'Vat ban all dis monkeyshining anyvay?' demanded Herr Syrup.

'Why, 'tis simple enough, 'tis,' said the major. 'Ye're well aware the rare earth praseodymium has high value, since 'tis of critical importance to a geegee engine. Now the asteroid—'

'*Ja*, I have read de proclamation. But vy did you have to land here at all? If Erse vants Lois, vy not attack Lois like honest men and not bodder my poor spaceship?'

McConnell frowned. ' 'Tis that would be the manly deed,' he admitted. 'Yit the opposition party, the Gaelic Socialists, may their cowardly souls fry in hell, happen to be in power at home, an' they won't sind the fleet ag'inst Laoighise; for the Anglians have placed heavy guard on it, in case of just such a frontal assault, an' that base ace of aggression holds our Republic in check, for it shall never be said we were the first to start a war.'

He tilted the flask to his lips again and embarked on a lengthy harangue. Herr Syrup extracted from this that the Shamrock League, the other important political party in the Erse Cluster, favored a more vigorous foreign policy: though its chiefs would not also have agreed to an open battle with the Anglian Navy. However, Scourge-of-the-Sassenach O'Toole was an extremist politician even for the League. He gathered men, weapons, and equipment, and set out unbeknownst to all on his own venture. His idea was first to occupy Grendel. This has been done without opposition; armed authority here consisted of one elderly constable with a truncheon. Of course, it was vital to keep the occupation unknown to the rest of the universe, since the Shamrock League Irredentist Expeditionary Force could not hope to fight off even a single gunboat sent from any regular fleet. The arrival of the *Mercury Girl* and the chance thus presented to announce a quarantine, was being celebrated up and down the inns of Grendel as unquestionably due to the personal intervention of good St. Patrick.

As for the longer-range scheme – oh, yes, the plan. Well, like most terraformed asteroids, Grendel had only a minimal gyrogravitic unit, powerful enough to give it a 24-hour rotational period (originally the little world had spun around once in three hours, which played the very devil with tea time) and an atmosphere retaining surface field of 980 cm./sec.^{2}. Maintaining that much attraction, warming up the iron mass enough to compensate for the sun's remoteness, and supplying electricity to the colonists, was as much as the Grendelian atomic-energy plant could do.

O'Toole's boys had brought along a geegee of awesome dimensions. Installed at the center of mass and set to repulsor-beam, this one would be able to move the entire planetoid from its orbit.

'Move it ag'inst Laoighise!' cried McConnell. 'An' we've heavy artillery mounted, too. Ah, what think ye of that, me boy? How long do ye think the Anglian Navy will stand up ag'inst a warcraft of this size? Eh? Ha, ha! Drink to the successful defense of Gaelic rights ag'inst wanton an' un-provoked aggression!'

'I t'ink maybe de Anglian Navy vait yust long enough to shoot two, t'ree atomic shells at you and den land de marines,' said Herr Syrup dubiously.

'Shell their own people livin' here?' answered McConnell. 'No, even the Sassenach are not that grisly. There'll not be a thing they can do but retire from the scene in all their ignominy. An' faith, whin we return home wi' poor auld lost Laoighise an' put her into her rightful orbit with the ither Erse Cluster worlds—'

'I t'ought her orbit vas orig'inally not de same as eider vun of your nations.'

'Exactly, sir. For the first time since the Creation, Laoi-ghise will be sailin' where the Creator intended. Well, then, all Erse will rise to support us, the craven Gaelic Socialist cabinet will fall an' the tide of victory sweep the Shamrock League to its proper place of government an' your humble servant to the Ministry of Astronautics, which same portfolio Premier-to-be O'Toole has promised me for me help. An' then ye'll see Erse argosies plyin' the deeps of space as never before in history – an' me the skipper of the half of 'em!'

'*Gud bevare's,*' said Herr Syrup.

McConnell rose with a bearlike bow at Emily, who had recovered enough composure to return into sight. 'Of course, Grendel will thin be returned to Anglia,' he said. 'But her one finest treasure she'll not bring home, a Stuart rose plucked to brighten a field of shamrocks.'

The girl lifted a brow and said coldly: 'Do I understand, Major, that you wish to keep me forever as a shield against the Anglian Navy?'

McConnell flushed. ' 'Tis the necessity of so usin' your

people that hurts every true Erse soul,' he said, 'an' be sure if it were not certain that no harm could come to the civilians here, we'd never have embarked on the adventure.' He brightened. 'An' faith, is it not well we did, since it has given me the sight of your sweet face?'

Emily turned her back and stamped one little foot.

'Also your sweet legs,' continued McConnell blandly, 'an' your sweet – er – Drink, Mister Syrup, drink up wi' me to the rightin' of wrongs an' the succorin' of the distressed!'

'Like me,' mumbled the engineer.

The girl whirled about. 'But people will be hurt!' she cried. 'Don't you understand? I've tried and tried to explain to you, my father's tried, everyone on Grendel has and none of you will listen! It's been forty years since our nations were last close enough together to have much contact. I mean, you just don't know how the situation has changed in Anglia. You think you can steal Lois, and our government will swallow a *fait accompli* rather than start a war – the way yours did when we first took it. But ours won't. Old King James died ten years ago. King Charles is a young man – a fire-eater – and the P.M. claims descent from Sir Winston Churchill – they won't accept it! I mean to say, your government will either have to repudiate you and give Lois back, or there'll be interplanetary war!'

'I think not, *acushla*, I think not,' said McConnell. 'Ye mustn't trouble your pretty head about these things.'

'I t'ink maybe she ban right,' said Herr Syrup. 'I ban in Anglia often times.'

'Well, if the Sassenach want a fight,' said McConnell merrily, 'a fight we'll give them!'

'But you'll kill so many innocent people,' protested Emily. 'Why, a bomb could destroy the Greek theatre on Scotia! And all for what? A little money and a mountain of pride!'

'*Ja*, you ruin my business,' croaked Sarmishkidu.

'And mine. My whole ship, said Herr Syrup, almost tearfully.

'Oh, now, now, now, man, ye at least should not be tryin' to blarney me,' said McConnell. 'What harm can a six or seven weeks' holiday here do to yez?'

'Ve ban carrying a load of Brahma bull embryos in exogenetic tanks,' said Herr Syrup. 'All de time, dose embryos is growing.' He banged his mug on the table. 'Dey is soon fetuses, by Yudas! Ve have only so much room aboard ship; and it takes time to reash Alamo from here. If ve are held up more dan two, t'ree veeks—'

'Oh, no!' whispered McConnell.

'*Ja*,' said Herr Syrup. 'Brahma bull calves all over de place. Ve cannot possibly carry dem, and dere is a stiff penalty in our contract.'

'Well, now.' McConnell looked uneasy. 'Sure, an' 'tis sorry I am, an' after this affair has all been settled, if yez wish to file a claim for damages at Teamhair I am sure the O'Toole government will— Oh, oh.' He stopped. 'Where did ye say your owners are?'

'Anguklukkakok City, Venus.'

Well—' Major McConnell stared at his toes, rather like a schoolboy caught in the cookie jar. 'Well, now, I meself think 'twas a good thing the Anguklukkakok Venusians were all converted last century, but truth 'tis, Jiniral O'Toole is pretty strict an'—'

'I say,' broke in Emily, 'what's the matter? I mean, if your owners are—'

'Baptists,' said Rory McConnell.

'Oh,' said Emily in a small voice.

McConnell leaped to his feet. One huge fist crashed on the table so the beer steins leaped. 'Well, 'tis sorry I am!' he shouted. Sarmishkidu flinched from the noise and folded up his ears. 'I've no ill will to anyone, meself, 'tis a dayd done for me country, an' – an' – an' why must all of yez be turnin' a skylarkin' merry-go into hurt an' harm an' sorrow?'

He stormed toward the exit.

'The score!' thundered Sarmishkidu in his thin, reedy voice. 'The score, you unevaluated partial derivative!'

McConnell ripped out his wallet, flung a five-pound note blindly on the floor, and went up the stairs three at a time. The door banged in his wake.

CHAPTER THREE

The sun was low when Knud Axel Syrup pedaled a slightly erratic course over the spaceport concrete. He had given the Alt Heidelberg several hours' worth of his business: partly because there was nothing else to do but work his way down the beer list, and partly because Miss Emily Croft – once her tears were dried – was pleasant company, even for a staid old married man from Simmerboelle. Not that he cared to listen to her exposition of Duncanite principles, but he had prevailed on her to demonstrate some classical dances. And she had been a sight worth watching, once he overcame his natural disappointment at learning that classical dance included neither bumps nor grinds, and found how to ignore Sarmishkidu's lyre and syrinx accompaniment.

'*Du skal faa min sofacykel naar jeg doer—*' sang Herr Syrup mournfully.

'An' what might that mean?' asked the green-clad guard posted beneath the *Mercury Girl*.

'*You shall have my old bicycle ven I die*,' translated Herr Syrup, always willing to oblige.

'*You shall have my old bicycle ven I die,*
    For de final kilometer
    Goes on tandem vit' St. Peter.
You shall have my old bicycle ven I die.'

'Oh, said the guard, rather coldly.

Herr Syrup leaned his vehicle against the berth. 'Dat is a

more modern verse,' he explained. 'De orig'inal song goes back to de T'irty Years' Var.'

'Oh.'

'Gustavus Adolphus' troops ban singing it as—' Something told Herr Syrup that his little venture into historical scholarship was not finding a very appreciative audience. He focused, with some slight difficulty, on the battered hull looming above him. 'Vy is dere no lights?' he asked. 'Is all de crew in town?'

'I don't know what,' confessed the guard. His manner thawed; he brought up his rifle and began picking his teeth with the bayonet. ' 'Twas a quare thing, begorra. Your skipper, the small wan in the dishcloth hat, was argyfyin' half the day wi' General O'Toole. At last he was all but thrown out of headquarters an' came back here. He found our boys just at the point of removin' the ship's radio. Well, now, sir, ye can see how we could not let ye live aboard your ship an' not see-questrate the apparatus by which ye might call New Winchester an' bring the King's bloody soldiers down on our heads. But no, that poor little dark sad man could not be reas'nable, he began whoopin' and screamin' for all his crew, an' off he rushed at the head of 'em. Now I ask ye, sir, is that any way to—'

Knud Axel Syrup scowled, fished out his pipe, and tamped it full with a calloused thumb. One could not deny, he thought, Captain Radhakrishnan was normally the mildest of human creatures; but he had his moments. He superheated, yes, that was what he did, he superheated without showing a sign, and then all at once some crucial thing happened and he flashed off in live steam and what resulted thereafter, that was only known to God and also the Lord.

'Heigh-ho,' sighed the engineer. 'Maybe someone like me vat is not so excited should go see if dere is any trouble.'

He lit his pipe, stuck it under his mustache, and climbed back onto his bicycle. Four roads led out of the spaceport, but one was toward town – so, which of three? – wait a minute. The crew would presumably not have stampeded quite at random. They would have intended to do something. What? Well, what would send the whole Shamrock League adventure downward and home? Sabotage of their new drive unit. And the asteroid's geegee installations lay down *that* road.

Herr Syrup pedaled quickly off. Twilight fell as he crossed the Cotswold Mountains, all of 500 meters high, and the gloom in Sherwood Forest was lightened only by his front-wheel lamp. But beyond lay open fields where a smoky blue dusk lingered, enough light to show him farmers' cottages and hayricks and – and – He put on a burst of speed.

The *Girl*'s crew were on the road, brandishing as wild an assortment of wrenches, mauls, and crowbars as Herr Syrup had ever seen. Half a dozen young Grendelian rustics milled about among them, armed with scythes and pitchforks. The whole band had stopped while Captain Radhakrishnan exhorted a pair of yeoman who had been hoeing a wayside cabbage patch and now leaned stolidly on their tools. As he panted closer, Herr Syrup heard one of them:

'Nay, lad, tha'll no get me to coom.'

'But, that is to say, but!' squeaked Captain Radhakrishnan. He jumped up and down, windmilling his arms. The last dayglow flashed off his monocle; it fell from his eye and he popped it back and cried: 'Well, but haven't you any courage? All we need to do, don't y' know, is destroy their geegee and they'll jolly well have to go home. I mean to say, we can do it ten minutes, once we've overcome whatever guards they have posted.'

'Posted wi' machine guns,' said the farmer.

'Aye,' nodded his mate. 'An' brass knuckles, Ah'll be bound.'

'But where's your patriotism?' shouted Captain Radhakrishnan. 'Imitate the action of the tiger! Stiffen the sinews, summon up the blood, disguise fair nature with hard-favour'd rage, and all that sort of thing.'

At this point Herr Syrup joined them. 'You ban crazy?' he demanded.

'Ah.' Captain Radhakrishnan turned to him and beamed. 'The very man. Come, let's leave these bally caitiffs and proceed.'

'But!' wailed Herr Syrup.

His assistant, Mr. Shubbish, nudged him with a tentacle and leered: 'I fixed up a Molotov cocktail, chief. Don't worry. We got it made.'

There was something in the air, a smell which – Herr Syrup's bulbous nose drank deep. Yes. Irish whisky. The crew must have spent a convivial afternoon with the spaceport sentries. So that explained why they were so eager!

'Miss Croft is right,' he muttered. 'About whisky, anyhow. It calcifies the liver.'

He pushed his bicycle along the road, beside Radhakrishnan's babbling commando, and tried to think of something which would turn them back. Eloquence was never his strong point. Could he borrow some telling phrase from the great poets of the past, to recall them to reason? But all that rose into his churning brain was the Death Song of Ragnar Lodhbrok, which consists of phrases like '*Where the swords were whining while they sundered helmets*' – and did not seem to fit his present needs.

Vaguely through dusk and a grove of trees, he saw the terraforming plant. And then the air whirred and a small flyer slipped above him. It hung for an instant, then pounced low and fired a machine-gun burst. The racket was unholily loud, and the tracer stream burned like meteorites.

'Oh, my goodness!' exclaimed Captain Radhakrishnan.

'Wait there!' bawled an amplified voice. 'Wait there an' we'll see what tricks ye're up to, ye Sassenach *omadhauns*!'

'Eek,' said Mr. Shubbish.

Herr Syrup ascertained that no one had been hit. As the flyer landed and disgorged more large Celts than he had thought even a spaceship could hold, he switched off his bicycle lamp and wheeled softly back out of the suddenly quiet and huddled rebel band. Crouched beneath a hedge-row, he heard a lusty bellow:

'An' what wad ye be a-doin' here, where 'tis forbidden to venture by order of the General?'

'We were just out for a walk,' said Captain Radhakrishnan, much subdued.

'Sure, sure. With weapons to catch the fresh air, no doubt.'

Herr Syrup stole from the shadows and began to pedal back the way he came. Words drifted after him. 'We'll jist see what himself has to say about this donnybrookin', me lads. Throw down your gear! 'Bout face! March!'

Herr Syrup pedaled a little faster. He would do no one any good languishing in the Grendel calaboose and living off mulligan stew.

Not, he thought gloomily, that he was accomplishing much so far.

The asteroid night deepened around him. In this shallow atmosphere the stars burned with wintry brilliance. Jupiter was not many millions of kilometers away, so whitely bright that Grendel's trees cast shadows; you could see the Galilean satellites with the naked eye. A quick green moon strode up over the topplingly close horizon and swung toward Aries – one of the other Anglian asteroids – spinning with its cluster mates around a common center of gravity, along a common resultant orbit. Probably New Winchester itself, maddeningly near. When you looked carefully at the sky, you could identify other little worlds among the constellations. The Erse Republic was still too remote to see without a telescope, but it was steadily sweeping closer; conjunction, two months hence, would bring it within a million kilometers of Anglia.

Herr Syrup, who was a bit of a bookworm, wondered in a wry way what Clausewitz or Halford Mackinder would think of modern astropolitics. Solemn covenants were all very well for countries which stayed put; but if you made a treaty with someone who would be on the other side of the sun next year, you must allow for the fact. There were alliances contingent on the phase of a moon and customs unions which existed only on alternate Augusts and—

And none of this was solving a problem which, if unsolved, risked a small but vicious interplanetary war and would most certainly put the *Mercury Girl* and the Alt Heideblerg Rathskeller out of business.

When he re-entered the spaceport, Herr Syrup met a blaze of lights and a bustle of men. Trucks rumbled back and forth, loaded with castings and fittings, sacks of cement and gangs of laborers. The Erse were working around the clock to make Grendel mobile. He dismounted and walked past a sentry, who gave him a suspicious glare, to the berth ladder, and so up to the air lock. He whistled a little tune as he climbed, trying to assure himself that no one could prove he had not merely been out on a spin for his health.

The ship was depressingly large and empty. His footsteps clanged so loud that he jumped, which only made matters worse, and peered nervously into shadowed corners. There was no good reason to stay aboard, he thought; an inn would be more cheerful and he could doubtless get off-season rates; but no, he had been a spaceman too long, one did not leave a ship completely unwatched. He contented himself with appropriating a case of Nashornbräu from the cargo – since the consignee had, after all, refused acceptance – and carried it back to his personal cubbyhole off the engine room.

Claus the crow blinked wicked black eyes at him from the bunk. '*Goddag,*' he said.

'*Goddag,*' said Herr Syrup, startled. To be courteously greeted by Claus was so rare that it was downright ominous.

'*Fanden hade dig!*' yelled the bird. '*Chameau!* Go stuff yourself, you scut! *Vaya al Diablo!*'

'Ah,' said Herr Syrup, relieved. 'Dat's more like it.'

He sat down on the bunk and pried the cap off a bottle and tilted it to his mouth. Claus hopped down and poked a beak in his coat pocket, looking for pretzels. Herr Syrup stroked the crow in an absent-minded way.

He wondered if Claus really was a mutant. Quite possibly. All ships carried a pet or two, cat or parrot or lizard or uglopender, to deal with insects and other small vermin, to test dubious air, and to keep the men company. Claus was the fourth of his spacefaring line; there had been radiation, both cosmic and atomic, in his ancestral history. To be sure, Earthside crows had always had a certain ability to talk, but Claus' vocabulary was fantastic and he was constantly adding to it. Also, could chance account for the selectivity which made most of his phrases pure billingsgate?

Well – there was a more urgent question. How to get a message to New Winchester? The *Girl*'s radio was carefully gutted. How about making a substitute on the sly, out of spare parts? No, O'Toole was not that kind of a dolt, he would have confiscated the spare parts as well, including even the radar.

But let's see. New Winchester was only some thousands of kilometers off. A spark-gap oscillator, powered by the ship's plant, could send an S.O.S. that far, even allowing for the inverse-square enfeeblement of an unbeamed broadcast. It would not be too hard to construct such an oscillator out of ordinary electrical stuff lying around the engine room. But it would take a while. Would O'Toole let Knud Axel Syrup tinker freely, day after day, in the captive ship? He would not.

Unless, of course, there was a legitimate reason to tinker. If there was some *other* job to be done, which Knud Axel Syrup could pretend to be doing while actually making a Marconi broadcaster. Only, there were competent engineers among the Erse. It would be strange if one of them, at least, did not inspect the work aboard the *Girl* from time to time. And such a man could not be told that an oscillator was a dreelsprail for the hypewangle camit.

So. Herr Syrup opened another bottle and recharged his pipe. One thing you must say for the Erse, given a trail of logic to follow, they follow it till the sun freezes over. Having mulled the question in his mind for an hour or two, Herr Syrup concluded that he could only get away with building an oscillator if he was in some place where no Erse engineer would come poking an unwelcome nose. So what was needed was an excuse to—

Along about midnight, Herr Syrup left his cabin and went into the engine room. Happily humming, he opened up the internal-field compensator which had so badly misbehaved on the trip down. Hm, hm, hm, let us see . . . yes, the trouble was there, a burned-out field coil, easily replaced . . . tum-te-tum-te-tum. Herr Syrup installed a coil of impedance calculated to unbalance the circuits. He shorted out two more coils, sprayed a variable condenser lightly with clear plastic, removed a handful of wiring and flushed it down the toilet, and spent an hour opening two big gas-filled rectifier tubes, injecting them with tobacco-juice vapor and resealing them. Having done which, he returned to his bunk, changed into night clothes, and took a copy of Kant's *Critique* off the shelf to read himself to sleep.

'Kraa, kraa, kraa,' grumbled Claus. 'Bloody foolishness, damme. *Pokker! Ungah, ungah!*'

CHAPTER FOUR

Inquiry in the morning established that the office of the Erse military commander had been set up in a requisitioned loft room downtown, above Miss Thirkell's Olde Giftie Shoppe. Shuddering his way past a shelf of particularly malignant-looking china dogs, Herr Syrup climbed a circular stair so quaint that he could barely squeeze his way along it. Half-way up, a small round man coming hastily down caromed off his paunch.

'I say!' exclaimed the small man, adjusting his pince-nez indignantly. He picked up his briefcase. '*Would* you mind backing down again and letting me past?'

'Vy don't you back up?' asked Herr Syrup in a harsh mood.

'My dear fellow,' said the small man, 'the right-of-way in a situation like this has been clearly established by Gooch vs. Torpenhow, Holm Assizes 2098, not to mention—'

Herr Syrup gave up and retreated. 'You is a lawyer?' he asked.

'A solicitor? Yes, I have the honor to be Thwickhammer of Stonefriend, Stonefriend, Thwickhammer, Thwickhammer, Thwickhammer, Thwickhammer, and Stonefriend, of Lincoln's Inn. My card, sir.' The little man cocked his head. 'I say, aren't you one of the spacemen who arrived yesterday?'

'*Ja.* I vas yust going to see about—'

'Don't bother, sir, don't bother. Beasts, that's all these invaders are, beasts with green tunics. When I heard of your crew's arrest, I resolved at once that they should not lack for legal representation, and went to see this O'Toole person. "Release them, sir," I demanded, "release them this instant on reasonable bail or I shall be forced to obtain a writ of habeas corpus".' Mr. Thwickhammer turned purple. 'Do you know what O'Toole told me I could do with such a writ? No, you cannot imagine what he said. He said—'

'I can imagine, *ja*,' interrupted Herr Syrup. Since they were now back in earshot of Miss Thirkell and the china dogs, he was spared explicit details.

'I am afraid your friends will be held in gaol until the end of the occupation,' said Mr. Thwickhammer. 'Beastly, sir. I have assured myself that the conditions of detention are not unduly uncomfortable, but really – I must say—!' He bowed. 'Good day, sir.'

Miss Thirkell looked wistfully at Herr Syrup, across the length of her deserted shoppe, and said: 'If you don't care for one of the little dogs, sir, I have some nice lampshades with "Souvenir of Grendel" and a copy of *Trees* printed on them.'

'No, t'ank you yust the same,' said Herr Syrup, and went quickly back upstairs. The thought of what an ax could do among all those Dresden shepherdesses and clock-bellied Venuses made him sympathize with his remote ancestors' practice of going berserk.

A sentry outside the office was leaning out the window, admiring Grendel's young ladies as they tripped by in their brief light dresses under a fresh morning breeze. Herr Syrup did not wish to interrupt him, but went quickly through the anteroom and the door beyond.

General Scourge-of-the-Sassenach O'Toole looked up from

a heap of papers on his desk. The long face tightened. Finally he clipped: 'So there ye are. An' who might have given ye an appointment?'

'*Ja*,' agreed Herr Syrup, sitting down.

'If 'tis about your spalpeen friends ye've come, waste no time. Ye'll not see thim released before Laoighise shall be free.'

'From de Shannon to de sea?'

'Says the Shan Van Vaught!' roared O'Toole automatically. He caught himself, snapped his mousetrap mouth shut, and glared.

'Er—' Herr Syrup gathered courage and rushed in. 'Ve have trouble on our ship. De internal compensator has developed enough bugs to valk avay vit' it. As long as ve is stranded here anyhow, you must let us make repairs.'

'Oh, must I?' murmured O'Toole, the glint of power in his eye.

'*Ja*, any distressed ship has got to be let fixed, according to de Convention of Luna. You vould not vant it said dat you vas a barbarian violating international law, vould you?'

General O'Toole snarled wordlessly. At last he flung back: 'But your crew broke the law first, actin' as belligerents when they was supposed to be neutrals. I've every right to hold them, accident to their ship or not, while the state of emergency obtains.'

Herr Syrup sighed. He had expected no more. 'At least you have no charge against me,' he said. 'I vas not any place near de trouble last night. So you got to let me repair de damage, no?'

O'Toole thrust a bony jaw at him. 'I've only your word there's any damage at all.'

'I knew you vould t'ink dat, so before I come here I asked you shief gyronics enshineer vould he please to look at our compensator and check it himself.' Herr Syrup unfolded a sheet of S.L.I.E.F. letterhead from his pocket. 'He gave me dis.'

O'Toole squinted at the green paper and read:

TO WHOM IT MAY CONCERN:

This is to say that I have personal inspected the internal field compensator of I/S *Mercury Girl* and made every test known to man. I certify that I have never seen any piece of apparatus so deranged. I further certify as my considered opinion that the devil has got into it and only Father Kelly can make the necessary repairs.

Shamus O'Banion
Col., Eng., S.L.I.E.F.

'Hm,' said O'Toole. 'Well, yes.'

'You realize I must take de ship up and put her in orbit outside Grendel's geegee field,' said Herr Syrup. 'I vill need freefall conditions to test and calibrate my repairs.'

'Yes!' O'Toole's arm shot out till his accusing finger was almost in the Dane's mustache. 'Let ye take the ship aloft so ye can sail it clear to New Winchester!'

Herr Syrup suppressed an impulse to bite. 'I expect you vill put a guard aboard,' he said. 'Yust some dumb soldier vat does not know enough about technics to be of any use to you down here.'

'Hm,' said O'Toole. 'Hm, hm, hm.' He gave the other man a malevolent glance. ' 'Tis nothin' but trouble I've had wi' the lot of yez,' he complained, 'an' sure I am in me heart ye're plottin' to make more. No, I'll not let ye do it. By the brogans of Brian Boru, here on the ground ye stay!'

Herr Syrup shrugged. 'Vell,' he said, 'if you vant all de Solar System to know later on how you vas breaking de Lunar Convention and not letting a poor old spaceman fix his ship like de law says he is entitled to – *ja*, I guess maybe de Erse Republic does not care vat odder countries t'ink about its civilization.'

'The devil take ye for a hairsplittin' wretch!' howled O'Toole. 'Sit there. Wait right there, me fine lad, an' if 'tis space law ye want, then space law ye'll get!'

His finger stabbed the desk communicator buttons. 'I want Captain Flanahan . . . No, no, no, ye leatherhead, I mean *Captain* Flanahan, the captain of the Shamrock League Irredentist Expeditionary Force's ship *Dies I.R.A.*!'

After an interchange of Gaelic, O'Toole snapped off the communicator and gave Herr Syrup a triumphant look. 'I've checked the space law,' he growled. ' 'Tis true ye're entitled to put your vessel in orbit if that's needful for your repairs. But I'm allowed to place a guard aboard her to protect our own legitimate interests; an' the guard is entitled not to hazard his life in an undermanned ship. Especially whin I legally can an' will take the precaution of impoundin' all the lifeboats an' propulsive units an' radios off the spacesuits, as well as the ship's radio an' radar which I have already got. So by the law, I cannot allow ye to lift with me guardsman aboard unliss ye've a crew iv at least three. An' your own crew is all in pokey, where I'm entitled to keep them till the conclusion of hostilities! Ha, ha, Mister Space Lawyer, an' how do ye like that?'

CHAPTER FIVE

Herr Syrup leaned his bicycle against the wall of the Alt Heidelberg and clumped downstairs. Sarmishkidu von Himmelschmidt hitched up his leather shorts and undulated to meet his guest. 'Grüss Gott,' he piped. 'And what will we have to drink today?'

'Potassium-40 cyanide on de rocks,' said the engineer moodily, lowering himself to a bench. 'Unless you can find me a pair of spacemen.'

'What for?' asked the Martian, drawing two mugs and sitting down.

Herr Syrup explained. Since he had to trust somebody somewhere along the line, he assumed Sarmishkidu would not blab what the real plan was, to construct a spark-gap transmitter and signal King Charles.

'Ach!' whistled the innkeeper. 'So! So you are actual trying to do somet'ings about this situation what is mine business about to ruin.' In a burst of sentiment, he cried out: 'I salute you, Herr Syrup! You are such a hero, I do not charge you for dis vun beer!'

'T'anks,' snapped the Dane. 'And now tell me vere to find two men I can use.'

'Hmmm. Now that is somewhat less susceptible to logical analysis.' Sarmishkidu rubbed his nose with an odd tentacle. 'It is truistic that we must axiomatize the problem. So, imprimis, there are no qualified Anglian spacemen on Grendel at the moment. The interasteroid lines all maintain their headquarters elsewhere. Secundus, while there are no active collaborationist elements in the population, the nature of its distribution in n-dimensional psychomathematical phase space implies that there would be considerable difficulty in finding suitable units of humanity, dH. The people of Grendel tend to be either stolid farmers, mechanics *und so weiter*, brave enough but too unimaginative to see the opportunities in your scheme, or else tourist-facility keepers whose lives have hardly qualified them to take risks. Those persons with enough fire and flexibility to be of use to you would probably lack discretion and might blurt out—'

'*Ja, ja, ja,*' said Herr Syrup. 'But dere are still several t'ousand people on dis asteroid. Among dem all dere must be some ready and able to, uh, strike a blow for freedom.'

'I am!' cried a clear young voice at the door, and Emily Croft tripped down the stairs, trailing vine leaves.

Herr Syrup started. 'Vat are you doing here?' he asked.

'I saw your bicycle outside,' said the girl, 'and, well, you were so sympathetic yesterday that I wanted to—' She hesitated, looking down at her small sandaled feet and biting a piquantly curved lip. 'I mean, maybe you were spreading pumpernickel with that awful Limburger cheese instead of achieving glowing health with dried prunes and other natural foods, but you were so nice about encouraging me to show you classical dance that I thought—'

Herr Syrup's pale eyes traveled up and down an assemblage of second through fifth order curves which, while a bit on the slender side of his own preferences, was far and away the most attractive sight he had encountered for a good many millions of kilometers. '*Ja,*' he said kindly. 'I am interested in such t'ings and I hope you vill show me more – Ahem!' He blushed. Emily blushed. 'I mean to say, Miss Croft, I have seldom seen so much – Vell, anyhow, later on, sure. But now please to run along. I have got to talk secrets vit' Herr von Himmelschmidt.'

Emily quivered. 'I heard what you said,' she whispered, large-eyed.

'You mean about making Grendel free?' asked Herr Syrup hopefully.

His hopes were fulfilled. She quivered again. 'Yes! Oh, but do you think, do you really think you can?'

He puffed himself and blew out his mustache. '*Ja*, I t'ink dere is a chance.' He buffed his nails, looked at them critically, and buffed them some more. 'I have my met'ods,' he said in his most mysterious accent.

'Oh, but that's wonderful!' caroled Emily, dancing over to take his arm. She put her face to his ear. 'What can I do?' she breathed.

'Vat? You? Vy, you must vait and—'

'Oh, no! Honestly! I mean to say, Mr. Syrup, I know all about spies and, and revolutions and interplanetary conspiracies and everything. Why, I found a technical error in *The Bride of the Spider* and wrote to the author about it and he wrote back the nicest letter admitting I was right and he hadn't read the book I cited. There was this old chap, you see, and this young chap, and the old chap had invented a death ray—'

'Look,' said Herr Syrup, 've is not got any deat' rays to vorry about. Ve have yust got somet'ing to do vat should not be known to very many folks before ve do it. Now you run on home and vait till it is all over vit'.'

Emily clouded up. She sniffed a tiny sniff. 'You don't think I can be trusted,' she accused.

'Vy, I never said dat, I only said—'

'You're just like all the rest.' She bent her golden head

43

and dabbed at her eyes. 'All of you. You either call me crazy, and believe those horrible lies about Miss Duncan's private life, and try to force things on me to calcify my liver, or you – you let me go on, I mean making a perfect ass of myself—'

'I never said you vas a perfect ass!' shouted Herr Syrup. He paused and reflected a moment. 'Aldough,' he murmured, 'you do have—'

'—and laugh at me behind my back, and, and, and, uh-h-h-h!' Emily took her face out of her hands, swallowed, sniffled, and turned drooping toward the stairs. 'Never mind,' she said disconsolately. 'I'll go. I know I bother you, I mean to say I'm sorry I do.'

'But – *pokker*, Miss Croft, I vas only—'

'One moment,' squeaked Sarmishkidu. 'Please! Wait a short interval of time dT, please, I have an idea.'

'Yes?' Emily pirouetted, smiling like sunshine through rain.

'I think,' said Sarmishkidu, 'we will do well to take the young lady into our confidence. Her discretion may not be infinite but her patriotism will superimpose caution. And, while she has not unduly encouraged any young men of Grendel during the period of my residence here, I am sure she must be far better acquainted with a far larger circle thereof than foreigners like you and me could ever hope to become. She can recommend whom you should approach with your plan. Is that not good?'

'By Yudas, *Ja*!' exclaimed Herr Syrup. 'I am sorry, Miss Croft. You really can help us. Sit down and have a glass of pure spring vater on me.'

Emily listened raptly as he unfolded his scheme. At the end, she sprang to her feet, threw herself onto Herr Syrup's lap, and embraced him heartily.

'Hoy!' he said, grabbing his pipe as it fell and brushing

hot coals off his jacket. 'Hoy, dis is lots of fun, but—'

'You have your crew right here already, you old silly,' the girl told him. 'Me.'

'*You?*'

'And Herr von Himmelschmidt, of course.' Emily beamed at the Martian.

'Eep!' said Sarmishkidu in horror.

Emily bounced back to her feet. 'But of course!' she warbled. 'Of course! Don't you see it? You can't get really-truly spacemen anyway, I mean a garageman or a chef couldn't help you in your real work, so why let the secret go further than it has already? I mean, dear old Sarmishkidu and I could hand you your spanner and your ape wrench and your abacus or whatever that long thin calculating thing is called, just as well as Mr. Groggins down at the sweet shop, and if there are any secret messages, why, we can talk to each other in Attic Greek. And I do make tea competently, Mum admits it, even though I never drink tea myself because it tans the kidneys or something, and I can take along some dried apricots and bananas and apples for myself and won't that terrible Major McConnell be just furious when he sees how we outsmarted him! Maybe then he will understand what all that whisky and bacon is doing to his brain, and will stop doing it and exercise himself in classical dance, because he really is quite graceful, don't you know—'

'Ooooh!' said Sarmishkidu. 'No, wait, wait, wait, *ach*, wait just one moment! We are not qualified spacemen anyhow so O'Toole does not accept us for a crew.'

'I t'ought dat over,' said Herr Syrup, 'and checked in de law books to make sure. In an emergency like dis, de highest ranking officer available, me, can deputize non-certified personnel, and dey vill have regular spacemen's standing vile de situation lasts. O'Toole vill eider have to let me raise

45

ship vit' you two or else release two of my shipmates.'

'Then you will take us along?' pounced Emily.

Herr Syrup shrugged. He might as well have a crew worth looking at. 'Sure,' he said. 'You is velcome.'

Sarmishkidu rolled his eyes uneasily. 'Better I stay on de ground. I got mine business to look after.'

'Oh, nonsense!' said Emily. 'If I go, we just about have to have a Martian for a chaperone, not that I don't trust Mr. Syrup because he really is a sweet old gentleman – oh, I'm sorry, Mr. Syrup, I didn't mean to make you wince – well, I mean to say, of course I'll have to go aboard without letting Father know or he would forbid me, but why distress the old dear afterward with the thought that even if I liberated Grendel I compromised my reputation? I mean, he is the vicar, you know, and it's been hard enough for him, my bringing home Duncanite teachings from Miss Carruthers' Select School for Young Ladies on Wilberforce. Though I didn't learn about it in class but from a lecture in the town hall which I happened to attend, and – And your tavern business, Mr. Sarmishkidu, isn't worth tuppence if we don't get rid of the Erse before vacation season begins, so won't you please come, there's a dear, or else I'll ask all my young men friends never to come in here again.'

Sarmishkidu groaned.

CHAPTER SIX

Herr Syrup halted his bicycle and Herr von Himmelschmidt untied his tentacles from around the baggage rack. A small bright sun shone through small bright clouds on Grendel's spaceport, the air blew soft and sweet, and even the old *Mercury Girl* looked a trifle less discouraged than usual. Not far away a truckload of Erse soldiers was bowling toward the geegee site to work, and however much one desired to throw them off this planetoid, one had to admit their young voices soared miraculously sweet.

'—*Ochone! Ochone! the men of Ulster cry.*
Ochone! Ochone! The lords an' ladies weepin'!
Dear, dear the man that nivver, nivver more shall be. Hoy, there, Paddy, see the colleen, ah, the brave broight soight iv her, whee-ee-whee-ew!'

The sentry at the ship berth slanted his rifle across Herr Syrup's path. 'Halt,' he said.

'Vat?' asked the engineer.

'Or I shoot,' explained the guard earnestly.

'Vat is dis?' protested Herr Syrup. 'I got a right on my own ship. I got de General's written permission, by yiminy, to take her up.'

'That's as may be,' said the guard, hefting his weapon, 'but I've me orders too, which is that ye're not trusted an' ye don't go aboard till your full crew *an'* the riprysintative of the Shamrock League is here.'

'Oh, vell, if dat is all,' said Herr Syrup, relieved, 'den here comes Miss Croft now, and I see a Erser beside her too.'

Still trailed by a receding tide of whistles, Emily came with long indignant strides across the concrete. She bore an outsize picnic basket which her green-clad escort kept trying to take for her. She would snatch it from him, stamp her foot, and try to leave him behind. Unfortunately, he was so big that her half-running pace was an easy amble for him.

Sarmishkidu squinted. 'By all warped Riemannian space,' he said at last, 'is that not Major McConnell?'

Herr Syrup's heart hit the ground with a dull thud.

'Ah, there, greetin's an' salutations!' boomed the large young man. 'An' accept me congratulations, sir, on choosin' the loveliest crew which ivver put to sky! Though truth 'tis, she might be just a trifle friendlier. Ah, but once up among the stars, who knows what may develop?'

'You don't mean you ban our guard?' choked Herr Syrup.

'Yes. An' 'tis guardsmanlike I look, eh, what?' beamed Rory McConnell, slapping the machine pistol and trench knife holstered at his belt, the tommy gun at his shoulder, and the rifle across his fifty-kilo field pack.

'But you ban needed down here!'

'Not so much, now that we're organized an' work is proceedin' on schedule.' McConnell winked. 'An' faith, when I heard what crew yez would have, sir, why, I knew at once where me real obligations lay. For 'tis five years an' more that me aged mither on Caer Dubh has plagued me to marry, that she may have grandchilder to brighten her auld age; so I am but doin' me filial duty.' He nudged Herr Syrup with a confidential thumb.

When the engineer had been picked up, dusted off, and apologized to, he objected: 'But does your chief, O'Toole, know you ban doing dis? I t'ought he would not like you associating vit' us.'

'O'Toole is somewhat of a fanatic,' admitted McConnell, 'but he gave me this assignment whin I asked for it. For ye understand, sir, he is not easy in the heart of him, as long as ye are in orbit with any chance whatsoever to quare his plans. So 'tis happiest he'll be, the soonest ye've finished your repairs an' returned here. Now I am certificated more as a pilot an' navigator than an injineer, but ye well know each department must be able to handle the work of t'other in emergency, so I will be able to give yez skilled assistance in your task. I've enough experience in geegees to know exactly what ye're doin'.'

'Guk,' said Sarmishkidu.

'What?' asked McConnell.

'I said, "Guk,"' answered Sarmishkidu in a chill voice, 'which was precisely my meaning.'

'All aboard!' bawled the Erseman, and went up the berth ladder two rungs at a time.

Emily hung back. 'I couldn't *do* anything about it,' she whispered, white-faced. 'He just insisted. I mean, I even hit him on the chest as hard as I could, and he grinned, you have to admit he's as strong as Herakles and if he would only study classical dance to improve his gait he would be nearly perfect.' She flushed. 'Physically, I mean, of course! But what I wanted to say is, shall we give up our plan?'

'No,' said Herr Syrup glumly, ''ve ban committed now. And maybe a chance comes to carry it out. Let's go.' He took his bicycle by the seat bar and dragged it up into the ship. No Dane is ever quite himself without a bicycle, though it is not true that all of them sleep with their machines. Fewer than ten percent do this.

He had been prepared to pilot the *Girl* into orbit himself, which was not beyond his training; but McConnell did it with so expert a touch that even the transition from geegee field to free fall was smooth. Once established in path, Herr Syrup jury-rigged a polarity reverser in the ship's propulsive circuits, to furnish weight again inside the hull. It was against regulations, since it immobilized the drive; and, of course, it lacked the self-adjustment of a true compensator. But this was a meteor-swept region, so there was no danger in floating inert; and, though neither spacemen nor asterites mind weightlessness *per se*, an attractive field always simplifies work. No one who has not toiled in free fall, swatting gobs of molten solder from his face while a mislaid screwdriver bobs off on its own merry way, has experienced the full perversity of matter.

'Ve can turn off de pull ven ve vish to test repairs,' said Herr Syrup.

Rory McConnell looked around the crowded engine room and the adjacent workshop. 'I envy yez this,' he said, with a bare touch of wistfulness. ' 'Tis spaceships are me proper place, an' not all this hellin' about wi' guns an' drums.'

'Er – *ja*.' Herr Syrup hesitated. 'Vell, you know, dere is really no reason to bodder you vit' de yob in here. Yust leave me to do it alone and – hm – *ja*,' he finished in a blaze of genius, 'go talk at Miss Croft.'

'Oh, I'll be doin' that, all right,' grinned McConnell, 'but I'd not be dallyin' about all the time whin another man was laborin'. No, I'll sweat over that slut of a machine right along wi' yez, Pop.' He raised one ruddy eyebrow above a wickedly blue sidelong glance. 'Also, I'll not be makin' of unsubstantiated accusations, but 'tis conceivable ye might not work on it yourself at all, at all, if left alone. Some might even imagine ye – oh – makin' a radio to call his bloody majesty. So, just to keep evil tongues from waggin', we'll retain all electrical equipment in here, an' here I meself will work an' sleep. Eh?' He gave Herr Syrup a comradely slap on the back.

'*Gott in Himmel*!' yelped Sarmishkidu from the passageway outside. 'What exploded in there?'

An arbitrary pattern of watches had been established to give the *Mercury Girl* some equivalent of night and day. After supper, which she had cooked, Emily Croft wandered up to the bridge while Sarmishkidu was simultaneously washing the dishes and mopping the galley floor. She stood gazing out the viewports for a long time.

Only feebly accelerated by Grendel's weak natural gravity, the ship would take more than a hundred hours to complete one orbit. At this distance, the asteroid filled seven degrees of sky, a clear and lovely half-moon, though only approximately spherical. On the dark part lay tiny twinkles of light, scattered farms and hamlets, the starlit sheen of Lake Alfred the Great. The town, its church on the doll-like edge of naked-eye visibility, its roofs making a ruddy blur, lay serene a bit west of the sunset line: tea time, she thought sentimentally, scones and marmalade before a crackling fire, and Dad and Mum trying not to show their worry about her. Then, dayward, marched the wide sweep of fields and woods under shifting cloud bands, the intense green of the fens, the Cotswolds and rustling Sherwood beyond. Grendel turned slowly against a crystal blackness set with stars, so many and so icily beautiful that she wanted to cry.

When she actually felt tears and saw the vision blur, she bit her lip. Crying wouldn't be British. It wouldn't even be Duncanite. Then she realized that the tears were due to a whiff from Herr Syrup's pipe.

The engineer slipped through the door and closed it behind him. 'Hist!' he warned hoarsely.

'Oh, go hist yourself!' snapped the girl. And then, in contrition: 'No, I'm sorry. A bad mood. I just don't know what to think.'

'*Ja*. I feel I am up in an alley myself.'

'Maybe it's the water aboard ship. It's tanked, isn't it? I mean, it doesn't come bubbling up from some mossy spring, does it?'

'No.'

'I thought not. I guess that's it. I mean, why I feel so mixed up inside, all sad and yet not really sad. Do you know what I mean? I'm afraid I don't myself.'

'Miss Croft,' said Herr Syrup, 've is in trouble.'

'Oh. You mean about Ro – about Major McConnell?'

'*Ja*. He has taken inventory of everyt'ing aboard. He has stowed all de electric stuffs in a cabinet vich he has locked, and he has de key, himself. How are ve going to make a broadcaster now?'

'Oh, damn Major McConnell!' cried Emily. 'I mean, damn him, actually!'

'Dere is a hope I can see,' said Herr Syrup. 'It vill depend on you.'

'Oh!' Emily brightened. 'Why, how wonderful! I mean, I was afraid it would be so dull, just waiting for you to— And I'm sorry to say it, but the ship is not very esthetic, I mean there's just white paint and all those clocks and dials and thingummies and really, I haven't found any books except things like *The Jovian Intersatellite Pilot with Ephemerides* or something else called *Pictures For Men*, where the women aren't in classical poses at all, I mean it's—' She broke off, confused. 'Where was I? Oh, yes, you wanted me to – But that's terrif! I mean, whee!' She jumped up and down, twirled till her tunic stood out horizontally and her wreath titled askew, and grabbed Herr Syrup's hands. 'What can I do? Do you want any secret messages translated into Greek?'

'No,' said the engineer. 'Not yust now. Uh ... er—' He stared down, blushing, and dug at the carpet with one square-toed boot. 'Vell, you see, Miss Croft, if McConnell got distracted from vorking on de compensator ... if he vas not in de machine shop vit' me very often, and den had his mind on somet'ing else ... I could pick de lock on de electrics box and sneak out de parts I need and carry on vit' our plan. But, vell, first he must be given some odder interest dat vill hold all his attention for several days.'

'Oh, dear,' said Emily. She laid a finger to her cheek. 'Let me think. What is he interested in? Well, he talks a lot about spaceships, he wanted to be an interplanetary explorer when this trouble is over, and, you know, he really is enthusiastic about that, why, he's so much like a little boy I want to rumple his hair—' She stopped, gulping. 'No. That won't do. I mean, the only person here who can talk to him about spaceships is yourself."

'I am afraid I am not yust exactly his type,' said Herr Syrup in an elaborate tone.

'I mean, *you* can't keep him distracted, because you're the one we want to have working behind his back,' said Emily. 'Let me see, what else? Yes, I believe Major McConnell mentioned being fond of poker. It's a card game, you know. And Mr Sarmishkidu is very interested in, uh, permutations. So maybe they could—'

'I am afraid Sarmishkidu is not yust exactly his type eider.' Herr Syrup frowned. 'For a young lady vat is so mad 'vit dat crazy Erser, you ban spending a lot of time vit' him to know his tastes so vell.'

Emily's face heated up. 'Don't you call me a collaborationist!' she shouted. 'Why, when the invaders first landed
I put on a Phrygian liberty cap and went around with a flag
calling on all our men to follow me and drive them off. And
nobody did. They said they had nothing more powerful than
a few shotguns. As if that made any difference!'

'It does make some difference,' said Herr Syrup placa-
tingly.

'But as for seeing Major McConnell since, why, how could
I help it? I mean, O'Toole made him the liaison officer for
us Grendelians, because even O'Toole must admit that Rory
has more charm. And naturally he had to discuss many
things with my father, who's one of Grendel's leading citizens, the vicar, you know. And while he was in our house,
well, he's a guest even if he is an enemy, and no Croft has
been impolite to a guest since Sir Hardman Croft showed a
Puritan constable the door in 1657. I mean, it just isn't done.
Of course I had to be nice to him. And he does have a lovely
soft voice, and any Duncanite appreciates musical qualities,
and that doesn't make me a collaborator, because I'd lead an
attack on their spaceship this very day if somebody would
only help me. And if I don't want any of them to get hurt,
why, I'm only thinking about their innocent parents and,
and sweethearts, and so there!'

'Oh,' said Herr Syrup.

His pipe had gone out. He became very busy rekindling it.
'Vell, Miss," he said, 'in dat case you vill help us out and try
to distract de mayor's mind off his vork, vill you not? It
ban your patriotic duty. Yust-encourashe-him-in-a-nice-vay-
because-he-is-really-in-love-vit'-you-okay? Good night.' And
hiding his beet-colored face in a cloud of smoke, Herr Syrup
bolted.

54

Emily stared after him. 'Why, good heavens,' she whispered. 'I mean, actually!'

Her eyes traveled back to Grendel and the stars. 'But that isn't so,' she protested. 'It's just what they call blarney. *Makros Logos* to be exact."

No one answered her for a moment, then feet resounded in the companionway and a hearty voice boomed: 'Emily, are ye up there?'

'Oh, dear!' exclaimed the girl. She looked around for a mirror, made do with a polished chrome surface, and adjusted her wreath and the yellow hair below it. She must not let a foreigner see an Anglian lady disarrayed, and really, she regretted not having any lipstick and felt sure that abstention from such materials didn't represent the true Duncanism.

Rory McConnell clumped in, his shoulders brushing the door jambs and his head stooped under the lintel. 'Ah, macushla, I found ye,' he said. 'Will ye not speek for a bit to a weary man, so he can sleep content? For even the hour or two of testin' I've been able to do today on that devil's machine has revealed nothin' to me but me own bafflement, an' 'tis consolation I need.'

Emily found herself breathing as hard as if she had run a long distance. *Oh, stop it!* she scolded. *Hyperventilating! No wonder you feel so weak and dizzy.*

The Erseman leaned close. For once he did not grin, he smiled, and it was not fair that a barbarian could have so tender a smile. 'Sure an' I never knew a pulse in any throat could be that adorable,' he murmured.

'Nice weather we're having, isn't it?' said Emily, since nothing else came to mind.

'The wither in space is always noice, though perhaps just a trifle monotonous,' quirked McConnell. He came around the pilot chair and stood beside her. The red hairs on the back of one hand brushed her bare thigh; she gulped and clung to the chair for support.

After all, her duty was to distract him. She was certain that even Isadora Duncan, the pure and serene, would have approved.

McConnell reached out a long arm and switched off the bridge lights, so that they stood in the soft, drenching radiance of Grendel, among a million stars. ''Tis enough to make a man believe in destiny,' he said.

'It is?' asked Emily. Her voice wobbled, and she berated herself. 'I mean, what is?'

'Crossin' space on this mission an' findin' ye waitin' at the yonder end. For I'll admit to yez what I've dared say to no one else, 'tis not important to me who owns that silly piece of ore Laoighise. I went with O'Toole because a McConnell has never hung back from any brave venture, arragh, how ye wring truth from me which I had not ayven admitted to meself! Oh, to be sure, I'm proud to do me country a service, but I cannot think 'tis so great an' holy a deed as O'Toole prates of. So I came more on impulse than plan, me darlin', an' yet I found me destiny. The which is your own sweet self.'

Emily's heart thumped with unreasonable violence. She clasped her hands tightly to her breast, because one of them had been sneaking toward McConnell's broad paw. 'Oh?' she said out of dry lips. 'I mean, really?'

'Yes. An' sorry I am that our work distresses yez. I can only hope to make amends later. But trust we'll have fifty or sixty years for that!'

'Er, yes,' said Emily.

'What?' roared McConnell. He spun on his heel, laid his

hands about her waist, and stared wildly down into her eyes. 'Did I hear ye say yes?'

'I ... I ... I – No, please listen to me!' wailed Emily, pushing against his chest. 'Let go! I mean, all I wanted to say was, if you don't really care how this business comes out, if you really don't think Lois is worth risking a war over and—' She drew a deep breath and tacked a smile on her face. Now was the time to distract him, as Mr. Syrup had requested. 'And if you really want to please me, R-r-r-ro— Major Mc-Connell, then why don't you help us right now? Just let us make that sparky osculator or whatever it is to call New Winchester for help, and everything will be so nice and – I mean—'

His hands fell to his sides and his mouth stretched tight. He turned from her, leaned on the instrument board and stared out at the constellations.

'No,' he said. 'I've given me oath to support the Force to the best of me ability. Did I turn on me comrades, there'd be worse than hellfire waitin' for me, there'd be the knowin' of meself for less than a man.'

Emily moistened her lips. There must be some way to distract him, she thought frantically. That beautiful lady agent in *The Son of the Spider*, the one who lured Sir Frederic Banton up to her apartment while the Octopus stole the secret papers from his office – She stood frozen among thunders, unable to bring herself to it, until another memory came, some pictures of an accidental atomic explosion of Callisto and its aftermath. That sort of thing might be done to little children, deliberately, if there was a war.

She stole up behind McConnell, laid her cheek against his back and her arms around his waist. 'Oh, Rory,' she said.

'What?' He spun around again. He was so quick on his feet she didn't have time to let go and was whipped around with him. 'Where are ye?' he called.

'Here,' she said, picking herself up.

She leaned on his arm – she had never before known a man who could take her whole weight thus without even stirring – and forced her eyes toward his. 'Oh, Rory,' she tried again.

'What do ye mean?' It was a disquieting surprise that he did not sweep her into his embrace, but stood rigidly and stared.

'Rory,' she said. Then, feeling that her conversation was too limited, she got out in a rush of words: 'Let's just forget all these awful things. I mean, let's just stay up here and, and, and I'll explain about Duncanism to you and, well, I mean don't go back to the engine room, please!'

He said in a rasp: 'So 'tis me ye'd be keepin' up here whilst auld Syrup does what he will in the stern? An' what do ye offer me besides conversation?'

'Everything!' said Emily, taking an automatic cue from the beautiful lady agent vs. Sir Frederic; because her own mind felt full of glue and hammers.

'Everything, eh?'

Suddenly his arm jerked from beneath her. She fell in a heap. The green-clad body towered above, up and up and *up*, and a voice like gunfire crashed:

'So that's the game, is it? So ye think I'd sell the honor of the McConnells for – for – Why, had I known yez for what ye are, I'd not have given yez a second look the third time we met. An' to think I wanted yez for the mother of me sons!'

'No,' cried Emily. She sat up, hearing herself call like a stranger across light-years. 'No, Rory, when I said everything I didn't mean everything! I just—'

'Never mind,' he snarled, and went from the bridge. The door cracked shut behind him.

CHAPTER SEVEN

Knud Axel Syrup paused a moment in the after transverse corridor. The bulkhead which faced him bore a stencilled KEEP OUT and three doors: the middle one directly to the engine room, the right-hand one to the machine shop, and the left to his small private cabin. These two side chambers also had doors opening directly on the engine room. It made for a lack of privacy distressing in the present cloak-and-dagger situation.

However, the wild Erseman would no doubt be up on the bridge for hours. Herr Syrup sighed, a little enviously, and went through the central door.

'Awwrk,' said Claus, flapping in from the cabin. '*Nom d'un nom d'une vache! Schweinhund! Sanamabiche!*'

'Exactly,' said Herr Syrup. He entered the little bathroom behind the main energy converter and extracted a bottle of beer from a cooler which he had installed himself. Claus paced impatiently along a rheostat. Herr Syrup crumbled a pretzel for him and poured a little beer into a saucer. The crow jabbed his beak into the liquid, tilted back his black head, shook out his feathers, and croaked: '*Gaudeamus igitur!*'

'You're velcome,' said Herr Syrup. He inspected the locked electrical cabinet. Duplicating a Yale key would call for delicate instruments and skilled labor. After latching all doors to the outside, he went into the machine shop, selected various items, and returned. First, perhaps, a wire into the slot. . . .

The main door shivered under a mule kick. Faintly through its insulated metal thickness came a harsh roar: 'Open up, ye auld scut, or I'll crack the outer hatches an' let ye choke!'

'Yumping Yupiter,' said Herr Syrup.

He pattered across the room and admitted Rory McConnell, who glared down upon him and snarled: 'So 'tis up to your sneakin' tricks ye are again, eh? Throw a pretty face an' long legs at me an' – Aaargh! Be off wi' yez!'

'But,' bleated Herr Syrup. 'But vas you not talkin' vit' Miss Croft?'

'I was,' said McConnell. ' 'Tis not a mistake I'll make ag'in. Go tell her to save her charms for bigger fools than me. I'm goin' to sleep now.' He tore off his various weapons, laid them beside his pack, and sat down on the floor. 'Git out!' he rapped, fumbling at a boot zipper. His face was like fire. 'Tomorry perhaps I can look at ye wi' out bokin'!'

'Oh, dear,' said Herr Syrup.

'Oh, shucks,' said Claus, though not in just those words.

Herr Syrup picked up his miscellaneous tools and stole back into the workshop. A moment afterward he remembered his bottle of beer and stuck his head back through the communicating door. McConnell threw a boot at him. Herr Syrup closed the door and toddled out to make another requisition on the cargo.

Having done so, he stopped by the saloon. Emily was there, her face in her arms, her body slumped over the table and shuddering with sobs. At the far end sat Sarmishkidu, puffing his Tyrolean pipe and making calculations.

'Oh, dear,' said Herr Syrup again, helplessly.

'Can you console her?' asked Sarmishkidu, rolling an eye

in his direction. 'I have endeavored to do so, and am sorry to report absolute failure.'

Herr Syrup took a strengthening pull from his bottle.

'You see,' explained the Martian, 'her noise distracts me.'

He fumed smoke for a dour moment. 'I should at least think,' he whined, 'that having dragged me here, away from my livelihood and all the small comforts which mean so much to a poor lonely exile among aliens like myself – sustaining, heartening consolations which already I find myself in sore need of – namely a table of elliptic integrals – having so ruthlessly forced me into the trackless depths of outer space, and apparently not even to any good purpose, she would have the consideration not to sit there and weep at me.'

'Dere, dere,' said Herr Syrup, patting the girl's shoulder.

'Uhhhhh,' said Emily.

'Dere, dere, dere,' continued Herr Syrup.

The girl raised streaming eyes and sobbed pathetically: 'Oh, go to hell.'

'Vat happened vit' you and de mayor?'

A bit startled, Emily sniffed out: 'Why, nothing, unless you mean that time last year when he asked me to preside at the Ladies' Potato Race, during the harvest festi— Oh! The Major!' She returned her face to her arm. 'Uhhhh-hoo-hoo-hoo!'

'I gather she tried to seduce him and failed,' said Sarmishkidu. 'Naturally, her professional pride is injured.'

Emily leaped to her feet. 'What do you mean, professional?' she screeched.

'*Warum*, nothing,' stammered Sarmishkidu, retreating into a different character. 'I just meant your female prides. All women are females by profession, *nicht war*? That is a

61

joke. Ha, ha,' he added, to make certain he would be understood.

'And I *didn't* try to – to – Oh!' Emily stormed out of the saloon. A string of firecracker Greek trailed after her.

'Vat is she saying?' gaped Herr Syrup.

Herr von Himmelschmidt turned pale. 'Please don't to ask,' he said. 'I did not know she was familiar with that edition of Aristophanes.'

'*Helledussel!*' said the engineer moodily. 'Ve ban hashed now.'

'Hmmm,' muttered Sarmishkidu. 'It is correct that the enemy is armed and we are not. Nevertheless, it is an observational datum that there are three of us and only one of him, and so if we could separate him from his weapons, even briefly, and—'

'And?'

'Oh. Well, nothing, I suppose.' Sarmishkidu brooded. 'True,' he said at last, 'one of him would still be equivalent to four or five of us.' He pounded the table with an indignant hand. Since the hand, being boneless, merely flopped when it struck, this was not very dramatic. 'It is most unfair of him,' he squeaked. 'Ganging up on us like that.'

Herr Syrup stiffened with thought.

'*Unlautere Wettbewerb*,' amplified the Martian.

'Do you know—' whispered the Dane.

'What?'

'I hate to do dis. It does not seem right. I know it is not right. But by Yoe, maybe he ban asleep now!'

The idea dawned on Sarmishkidu. 'Well, I'll be an unelegantly proven lemma,' he breathed. 'So he doubtless is.'

'And for veapons, in de machine shop is all de tools. Like wrenches, hammers, vire cable—'

'Blowtorches,' added Sarmishkidu eagerly. 'Hacksaws, sulfuric acid—'

'No, hoy, vait dere! Just a minute! I don't vant to hurt him. Yust a little bonk on de head to make him sleep sounder, vile ve tie him up, dat's all.' Herr Syrup leaped erect. 'Let's go!'

'Good luck,' said Sarmishkidu, returning to his calculations.

'Vat? But hey! Is you leaving me to do dis all alone?'

Sarmishkidu looked up. 'Go!' he said in a ringing croak. 'Remember the Vikings! Remember Gustavus Adolphus! Remember King Christian standing by the high mast in smoke and steam! The blood of heroes is in your veins. Go, go to glory!'

Fired, Herr Syrup started for the door. He stopped there and asked wistfully, 'Don't you vant a little glory too?'

Sarmishkidu blew a smoke ring and scribbled an equation. 'I am more the intellectual type,' he said.

'Oh.' Herr Syrup sighed and went down the corridors. His resolution endured till he actually stood in the workshop, by the glow of a dim night light, hefting a pipe wrench. Then he wavered.

The sound of deep, regular breathing assured him that Major McConnell slept in the adjoining bedchamber. But— 'I don't vant to hurt him,' repeated Herr Syrup. 'I could so easy clop him too hard.' He shuddered. 'Or not hard enough. I better make another requisition on de cargo first. ... No. Here ve go.' Puffing out his mustache and mopping the sweat off his pate, the descendant of Vikings tiptoed into the engine room.

Rory McConnell would scarcely have been visible at all, had his taste in pajamas not run to iridescent synthesilc embroidered with tiny shamrocks. As it was, his body, sprawled on a military bedroll, seemed in the murk to stretch on and on, interminably, besides having more breadth and thickness than was fair in anything but a gorilla. Herr Syrup hunkered shakily down by the massive red head, squinted till he had a spot, just behind one ear identified, and raised his weapon.

There was a snick of metal. The wan light glimmered along a pistol barrel. It prodded Herr Syrup's nose. He let out a yelp and broke all Olympic records for the squatting high jump.

Rory McConnell chuckled. 'I'm a sound sleeper when no one else comes sneakin' close to me,' he said, 'but I've hunted in too many forests not to awaken thin. Goodnight, Mister Syrup.'

'Goodnight,' said Knud Axel Syrup in a low voice.

Blushing, he went back to the machine room. He waited there a moment, ashamed to return to his cabin past Mc-Connell and yet angry that he must detour. Oh, the devil with it! He heard the slow breath of slumber resume. Viciously, he slammed his tool back into the rack loudly enough to wake an estivating Venusian. The sleeper did not even stir. And that was the unkindest cut of all.

Stamping his feet, slamming doors, and kicking panels as he went by – all without so much as breaking the calm rhythm of Rory McConnell's lungs – Herr Syrup took the roundabout way to his cabin. He switched on the light and pointed a finger at Claus. The crow hopped off the Selected Works of Oehlenschläger and perched on the finger.

'Claus,' said Herr Syrup, not quite bellowing, 'repeat after me: McConnell is a louse. McConnell is no good. McConnel eats vorms. On Friday. McConnell—'

—slept on.

Herr Syrup decided at last to retire himself. With a final

sentence for Claus to memorize, an opinion in crude language of Major McConnell's pajamas, he took off his own clothes and slipped a candy-striped nightshirt over his head. Stretched out in his bunk, he counted herrings for a full half hour before realizing that he was more awake than ever.

'*Satans ogsaa,*' he mumbled, and switched on the light and reached at random for a book. It turned out to be a poetry anthology. He opened it and read:

'—*The secret workings of the yeast of life.*'

'Yudas,' he groaned. 'Yeast.'

For a moment Herr Syrup, though ordinarily the gentlest of men, entertained bloodshot fantasies of turning the ship's atomic-hydrogen torch into a sort of science fiction blaster and burning Major McConnell down. Then he decided that it was impractical and that all he could do was requisition a case of lager and thus get to sleep. Or at least pass the night watch more agreeably. He decorated his feet with outsize slippers and padded into the corridor.

Emily Croft jumped. 'Oh!' she squeaked, whipping her robe about her. The engineer brightened a little, having glimpsed that her own taste in sleeping apparel ran merely to what nature had provided.

'Vich is sure better dan little green clovers,' he muttered.

'Oh . . . you startled me.' The girl blinked. 'What did you say?'

'Dat crook in dere.' Herr Syrup jerked a splay thumb at the engine room door. 'He goes to bed in shiny payamas vit' shamrocks measled all over.'

'Oh, dear,' said Emily. 'I hope his wife can teach him—' She skidded to a halt and blushed. 'I mean, if any woman would be so foolish as to have such a big oaf.'

'I doubt it,' snarled the Dane. 'I bet he snores.'

'He does not!' Emily stamped her foot.

'Oh-ho,' said Herr Syrup. 'You ban listening?'

'I was only out for a constitutional in the hope of overcoming an unfortunate insomnia,' said Miss Croft primly. 'It was sheer chance which took me past here. I mean, nobody who can lie there like a pig and, and sleep when—' She clouded up for a rainstorm. 'I mean, how *could* he?'

'Vell, but you don't care about him anyvay, do you?'

'Of course not! I hope he rots, I mean decays. No, I don't actually mean that, you know, because even if he is an awful lout he is still a human being and, well, I would just like to teach him a lesson. I mean, teach him to have more consideration for others and not go right to sleep as if nothing at all had happened, because I could see that he was hurt and if he had only given me a chance to explain, I – Oh, never mind!' Emily clenched her fists and stamped her foot again. 'I'd just like to lock him up in there, since he's sleeping so soundly. That would teach him that other people have feelings even if he doesn't!'

Herr Syrup's jaw dropped with an audible clank.

Emily's eyes widened. One small hand stole to her mouth. 'Oh,' she said, 'is anything wrong?'

'By yiminy,' whispered Herr Syrup. 'By yumping yiminy.'

'Oh, really now, it isn't that bad. I mean, I know we're in an awful pickle and all that sort of thing, but really—'

'No. I got it figured. I got a vay to get de Erser off of our necks!'

'What?'

'*Ja, ja, ja*, it is so simple I could beat my old knucklebone brains dat I don't t'ink of it right avay. Look, so long as ve stay out of de engine room he sleeps yust like de dummy in a bridge game vaiting for de last trump. No? Okay, so I close all de doors to him, dere is only t'ree, dis main vun and vun to my cabin and vun to de vorkshop. I close dem and veld dem shut and dere he is!'

Emily gasped.

She leaned forward and kissed him.

'Yudas priest,' murmured Herr Syrup faintly. His revolving eyeballs slowed and he licked his lips. 'T'ank you very kind,' he said.

'You're wonderful!' glowed Emily, brushing mustache hairs off her nose.

And then, suddenly: 'No. No, we can't. I mean, he'll be right in there with the machinery and if he turns it off—'

'Dat's okay. All de generators and t'ings is locked in deir shieldings, and dose keys I have got.' Herr Syrup stumped quickly down the hall and into the machine shop. 'His gun does him no good behind velded alloy plating.' He selected a torch, plugged it in, and checked the current. 'So. Please to hand me dat helmet and apron and dose gloves. Don't look bare-eyed at de flame.'

Gently, he closed the side door. Momentarily he was terrified that McConnell would awaken: not that the Erseman would do him any harm, but the scoundrel was so unfairly large. However, even the reek of burning paint, which sent Emily gagging back into the corridor, failed to stir him.

Herr Syrup plugged his torch to a drum of extension cord and trailed after her. 'Tum-te-tum-te-tum,' he warbled, attacking the main door. 'How does dat old American vork song go? Yohn Henry said to de captain, Vell, a man ain't not'ig but a man, but before I umpty-tumty-somet'ing-somet'ing, I'll die vit' a somet'ing-umpty-tum, Lord, Lord, I'll die vit' a tiddly-tiddly-pom!' He finished the job. 'And now to my cabin, and ve is t'rough.'

Emily's mouth quivered. 'I do hate to do this,' she said. 'I mean, he is such a darling. No, of course he isn't, I mean he's an oaf, but – not really an oaf either, he just has never had a chance to – Oh, you know what I mean! And now he'll be shut away in there, all alone, for days and days and days.'

Herr Syrup paused. 'You can talk to him on de intercom,' he suggested.

'What?' She elevated her nose. 'That big lout? *Let* him sit all alone! Maybe then he can see there are other people in the universe besides himself!'

Herr Syrup entered his cabin and began to close the inner door.

'McConnell is a four-lettering love child!' screamed Claus.

'He is not either!' yelled Emily, turning red.

There was a stir in the engine-room darkness. 'What's all that racket out there?' complained a lilting basso. 'Is it not enough to break me heart, ye must keep me from the sleep which is me one remainin' comfort?'

'Sorry,' said Herr Syrup, and closed the door.

'Hey, there!' bawled McConnell. He bounced off his bedroll. The vibration of it shivered in the metal. 'What's going on?'

'Yust lie down,' babbled Herr Syrup. 'Go back to sleep.' His cracked baritone soared as he switched on the torch. Sparks showered about him. '*Lullaby-y-y and good night, dy-y-y mo-o-o-der's deli-ight—*'

'Ah, ha!' McConnell thundered toward the door. 'So 'tis cannin' me ye are, ye treacherous Black-an'-Tanners! We'll see about that!'

'Look out!' screamed Emily. 'Look out, Rory! It's hot!'

A torrent of Gaelic oaths, which made Claus gape in awe, informed her that McConnell had discovered this for himself. Herr Syrup played the flame up and down and crossways. A tommy gun rattled on the other side, but the *Girl*, though old, was of good solid construction, and nothing happened but a nasty spang of ricochet.

'Don't!' pleaded Emily. 'Don't, Rory! You'll kill yourself! Oh, Rory, be careful!'

Herr Syrup cut off his torch, slapped back his helmet, and looked with enormous self-congratulation at the slowly cooling seams. 'Dere, now,' he said. 'Dat's dat!'

Claus squawked. The engineer turned around just in time to see his bunk blankets spring up in flame.

Emily leaned against the wall and cried through smoke and fire extinguisher fumes: 'Rory, Rory! Are you all right, Rory?'

'Oh, yes, I'm alive,' growled the voice behind the panels. 'It pleases ye better to let me thirst an' starve to death in here than kill me honestly, eh?'

'*Ou ma Dia!*' gasped the girl. 'I didn't think of that!'

'Yes, yes. Tell it to the King's marines.'

'Just a minute!' she begged, frantic. 'Just a minute and I'll get you out! Rory, I swear I never— Look out, I'll have to cut the door open—'

Herr Syrup dropped the plastifoam extinguisher and clapped a hand on her wrist as she picked up the torch. 'Vat you ban doing?' he yelped.

'I've got to release him!' cried Emily. 'We've got to! He hasn't anything in there to keep him alive!'

Herr Syrup gave her a long stare. 'So you t'ink his life is vort' more dan all de folk vat maybe get killed if dere is a var, huh?' he asked slowly.

'Yes . . . no . . . oh, I don't know!' sobbed the girl, struggling in his grasp and kicking at his ankles. 'We've got to let him out, that's all!'

'Now vait, vait yust a minute. I t'ought of dis problem right avay. It is not so hard. Dere is ventilator shafts running all t'rough de ship, maybe ten centimeters diameter. Ve yust unscrew a fan in vun and drop down cans of space rations to him. And a can opener, natural. It vill not hurt him to eat cold beans and drink beer for a vile. He has also got a bat'room in dere, and I t'ink a pack of cards. He vill be okay.'

'Oh, thank God!' whispered Emily.

She put her lips close to the door and called: 'Did you hear that, Rory? We'll send you food through the ventilator. And don't worry about it being just cold beans. I mean, I'll make you nice hot lunches and wrap them well so you can get them intact. I'm not a bad cook, Rory, honestly, I'll prove it to you. Oh, and do you have a razor? Otherwise I'll find one for you. I mean, you don't want to come out all bristly – I mean – oh, never mind!'

'So,' rumbled the prisoner. 'Yes, I heard.' Suddenly he shouted with laughter. 'Ah, t'is sweet of yez, darlin', but it won't be needful. Ye'll be releasin' me in a day or two at the most.'

Herr Syrup started and glared at the door. 'Vat's dat?' he snapped.

'Why, t'is simple 'tis. For the lifeboats are down on Grendel, an' even the propulsive units of every spacesuit aboard, not to speak of the radio an' radar, an' the spare electrical parts is all in here with me. An' so, for the matter of it, is the engines. Ye can't get the King's help, ye can't even get back to ground, without a by-your-leave from me. So I'll expect ye to open the door in as few hours as it takes for that fact to sink home into the square head of yez. Haw, haw, haw!'

'*Det var some fanden,*' said the engineer.

'What?'

'De hell you say. I got to look into dis.' Herr Syrup scurried from the cabin, his nightgown flapping about his hairy shanks and the forgotten fire extinguisher still jetting plasti-foam on the floor behind him.

'Oh, dear.' Emily wrung her hands. 'We just don't have any luck.'

McConnell's voice came back: 'Never mind, macushla, for I heard how ye feared for me life, an' that at a moment whin ye thought ye'd the upper hand. So 'tis humbly I ask your pardon for all I said earlier this night. 'Twas a good trick ye've played on me now, even if it did not work, an' many a long winter evenin' we'll while away in after years a-laughin' at it.'

'Oh, Rory!' breathed Emily, leaning against the door.

'Oh, Emily!' breathed McConnell on his side.

'Rory!' whispered the girl, closing her eyes.

The unnoticed plastifoam crept up toward her ears.

CHAPTER EIGHT

Sarmishkidu slithered into the Number Three hold and found Herr Syrup huddled gloomily beneath one of the enormous beer casks. He had a mug in one hand and the tap of the keg in the other. Claus perched on a rack muttering: 'Damn Rory McConnell. Damn anybody who von't damn Rory McConnell. Damn anybody who von't sit up all night damning Rory McConnell.'

'Oh, there you are,' said the Martian. 'Your breakfast has gotten cold.'

'I don't vant no breakfast,' said Herr Syrup. He tossed off his mug and tapped it full again.

'Not even after your triumph last watch?'

'Vat good is a triumph ven I ain't triumphant? I have sealed him into de engine room, *jo*, vich is to say ve can't move de ship from dis orbit. You see, de polarity reverser vich I installed on de geegee lines, to give us veight, is in dere vit' him, and ve can't travel till it has been taken out again. So ve can't go direct to New Vinshester ourselves. And he has also de electrical parts locked up vit' him.'

'I have never sullied my mathematics with any attempt at a merely practical application,' said Sarmishkidu piously, 'but I have studied electromagnetic theory and it would appear upon integration of the Maxwell equations that you could rip out wires here and there, machine the bar and plate metal stored for repair work in the shop, and thus improvise an oscillator.'

'Sure,' said Herr Syrup. 'Dat is easy. But remember, New Vinshester is about ten t'ousand kilometers avay. Any little laboratory model powered yust off a 220-volt line to some cabin, is not going to carry a broadcast dat far. At least, not vun vich has a reasonable shance of being noticed dere in all de cosmic noise. I do have access to some powerful batteries. By discharging dem very quick, ve can send a strong signal: but short-lived, so it is not likely in so little a time dat anyvun on de capital asteroid is listening in on dat particular vavelengt'. For you see, vit'out de calibrated standards and meters vich McConnell has, I cannot control de freqvency vich no vun of New Vinshester's small population uses or is tuned in on.'

He sighed. 'No, I have spent de night trying to figure out somet'ing, and all I get is de answer I had before. To make an S.O.S. dat vill have any measurable shance of being heard, ve shall have to have good cable, good impedances, meters and so on – vich McConnell is now sitting on. Or else ve shall have to run for a long time t'rough many unknown freqvencies, to be sure of getting at least vun vich will be heard; and for dat ve shall have to use de enshine room g'enerator, vich McConnell is also sitting on.'

'He is?' Sarmishkidu brightened. 'But it puts out a good many thousands of volts, doesn't it?'

'I vas speaking figurative, damn de luck.' Herr Syrup put the beer mug to his lips, lifted his mustache out of the way with a practiced forefinger, and bobbed his Adam's apple for a while.

Sarmishkidu folded his walking tentacles and let down his

73

bulbous body. He waggled his ears, rolled his eyeballs, and protested: 'But we can't give up yet! We just can't. Here iss all dis beautiful beer that I could sell at fifty percent profit, even if I have the pretzels und popcorn free. And what good is it doing? None!'

'Oh, I vouldn't say dat,' answered Herr Syrup, a trifle blearily, and drew another mugful.

'Dis lot has too much carbonation for my taste,' he complained. 'You t'ink I ban an American? It makes too much head.'

'That's on special order from me,' confided the Martian. 'In the head is the profit, if one is not too generous in scraping it off.'

'You is got too many arms and not enough soul,' said Herr Syrup. 'I t'ink for dat I let you clean out my cabin. It is got full vit' congealed plastifoam. And to make a new fire extingvisher for it, vy, I take a bottle of your too carbonated beer and if dere is a fire I shake it and take my t'umb off de mout' and— Of course!' mused Herr Syrup, 'could be you got so much CO_2 coming out, I get t'rown backwards.'

'If you don't like my beer,' said Sarmishkidu, half closing his eyes, 'you can just let me have the stein you got.'

'Action and reaction,' said Herr Syrup.

'Hm?'

'Newton's t'ird law.'

'Yes, yes, yes, but what relevance does that have to—'

'Beer. I shoot beer out de front end of de bottle, I get tossed on my can.'

'But you said it was a bottle.'

'*Ja, ja, ja, ja—*'

'*Weiss' nicht wie gut ich dir bin?*' sang the Martian.

'I mean,' said Herr Syrup, wagging a solemn finger, 'de bottle is a kind of rocket. Vy, it could even – it could even—'

74

His voice ground to a halt. The mug dropped from his hand and splashed on the floor.

'Beerslayer!' screamed Claus.

'But darlin',' said Rory McConnell into the intercom, 'I don't like dried apricots.'

'Oh, hush,' said Emily Croft from the galley. 'You've never been healthier in your life.'

'I feel like I'm rottin' away. Not through the monotony so much, me sweet, whilst I can be hearin' the soft voice of yez, but the only exercise I can get is calisthinics, which has always bored me grievous.'

'True,' said Emily, 'all those fuel pipes and things don't leave much room for classical dancing, do they? Poor dear!'

'I'd trade me mother's brown pig for a walk in the rain wi' yez, macushla.'

'Well, if you'd only give us your parole not to make trouble, dear, we could let you out this minute.'

'No, ye well know the Force has me prior oath an' the Force I'll fight for till 'tis disbanded either through victory or defeat. An' how long will it take the auld *omadhaun* Syrup to realize 'tis him has been defayted? I've lain in here almost a week be the clock. I hear noises day an' night from the machine room, an' devil a word I can get of what's goin' on. Let me out, swateheart! I bear no ill will. I'll kiss the pretty lips of ye an' we'll all go down to Grendel an' say nothin' about what's happened. Save of course that I've won the loveliest girl in the galaxy for me own.'

'I wish I could,' sighed Emily. 'How I wish it! *O Dion who sent my heart mad with love!*'

'Who's this Dion?' bristled Major McConnell.

'Nobody you need worry about, dear. It's only a quotation. Translated, naturally. But what I mean to say is, Mr.

Syrup and Mr. Sarmishkidu have so much to take care of and it won't be long now, I swear it won't, just another day or two, they say, and then their project will be over and they can – Oh! I promised not to tell! But what I mean, dear, is that I'll stay behind and I'm not supposed to let you out immediately, maybe not for still another day, but I'll look after you and make you nice lunches and – Yes,' said Emily with a slight shudder, 'there won't even be any more dried fruit in your meals, because I've run out of what there was; in fact, for days now I've been giving it all to you and eating corned beef and drinking beer myself, and I must admit it tastes better than I remembered, so if you insist on calcifying your liver after we're married, why, I suppose I'll have to also, and actually, darling, I don't know anyone who I'd rather calcify my liver with. Really.'

'What is all this?' Rory McConnell stepped back, his big frame tensing. 'Ye mean they've not just been putterin' about, but have some plan?'

'I mustn't tell! Please, beloved, honestly, I've been sworn to absolute secrecy, and now I must go. They need me to help too. I have been installing pipe lines and things and actually, dear, it's very exciting. I mean, when I use a welding torch I have to wear a helmet very much like a classical dramatic mask, so I stand there reciting from the *Agamemnon* as if I were on a real Athenian stage, and do you know, I think when this is all over and we're married and have our own Greek theater in the garden I'll organize a presentation of the whole *Orestes* trilogy – in the original, of course – with welding outfits. 'Bye now!' Emily blew a kiss down the intercom and pattered off.

Rory McConnell sat down on a generator shield and began most furiously to think.

CHAPTER NINE

The first beer-powered spaceship in history rested beneath a derrick by the main cargo hatch.

It was not as impressive as Herr Syrup could have wished. Using a small traveling lift for the heavy work, he had joined four ten-ton casks of Nashornbräu end to end with a light framework. The taps had been removed from the kegs and their bungholes plugged, simple electrically-controlled Venturi valves in the plumb center being substituted. Jutting on orthogonal axes from each barrel there were also L-shaped exhaust pipes, by which it was hoped to control rotation and sideways motion. Various wires and shafts, their points of entry sealed with gunk, plunged into the barrels, ending in electric beaters. A set of relays was intended to release each container as it was exhausted. The power for all this – it did not amount to much – came from a system of heavy-duty EXW batteries at the front end.

Ahead of those batteries was fastened a box, some two meters square and three meters long. Sheets of plastic were set in its black-painted sides by way of windows. The torso and helmet of a spacesuit jutted from the roof, removably fastened in a screwthreaded hatch cover which could be turned around. Beside it was a small stovepipe valve holding two self-closing elastic diaphragms through which tools could be pushed without undue air loss. The box had been put together out of cardboard beer cases, bolted to a light metal frame and carefully sized and gunked.

'You see,' Herr Syrup had explained grandly, 'in dis situation, vat do ve need to go to New Vinshester? Not an atomic motor, for sure, because dere is almost negligible gravity to overcome. Not a nice streamlined shape, because ve have no air hereabouts. Not great structural strengt', for dere is no strain odder dan a very easy acceleration; so beer cardboard is strong enough for two, t'ree men to sit on a box of it under Eart' gravity. Not a fancy t'ermostatic system for so short a hop, for de sun is far avay, our own bodies make heat and losing dat heat by radiation is a slow process. If it does get too hot inside, ve can let a little vater evaporate into space t'rough de stovepipe to cool us; if ve get chilly, ve can tap a little heat t'rough a coil off de batteries.

'All ve need is air. Not even much air, since I is sitting most of de time and you ban a Martian. A pair of oxygen cylinders should make more dan enough; ja, and ve vill need a chemical carbon-dioxide absorber, and some dessicating stuffs so you do not get a vater vapor drunk. For comfort ve vill take along a few bottles beer and some pretzels to nibble on.

'As for de minimal boat itself, I have tested de exhaust velocity of hot, agitated beer against vacuum, and it is enough to accelerate us to a few hundred kilometers per hour, maybe t'ree hundred, if ve use a high enough mass ratio. And ve vill need a few simple navigating instruments, an ephemeris, slide rule, and so on. As a precaution, I install my bicycle in de cabin, hooked to a simple home-made generator, yust a little electric motor yuggled around to be run in reverse, vit' a rectifier. Dat vay, if de batteries get too veek ve can recharge dem. And also a small, primitive oscillator ve can make, short range, ja, but able to run a gamut of frequencies vit'out exhausting de batteries, so ve can send an S.O.S. ven ve ban qvite close to New Vinshester. Dey hear it and send a space-ship out to pick us up, and dat is dat.'

The execution of this theory had been somewhat more difficult, but Herr Syrup's years aboard the *Mercury Girl* had made him a highly skilled improviser and jackleg inventor. Now, tired, greasy, and content, he smoked a well-earned pipe as he stood admiring his creation. Partly, he waited for the electric coils which surrounded the boat and tapped the ship's power lines, to heat the beer sufficiently; but that was very nearly complete, to the point of unsafeness. And partly he waited for the ship to reach that orbital point which would give his boat full tangential velocity toward the goal; that would be in a couple of hours.

'Er . . . are you sure we had better not test it first?' asked Sarmishkidu uneasily.

'No, I t'ink not,' said Herr Syrup. 'First, it vould take too long to fix up an extra barrel. Ve been up here a veek or more vit'out a vord to Grendel. If O'Toole gets suspicious and looks t'rough a telescope and sees us scooting around, right avay he sends up a lifeboat full of soldiers; vich is a second reason for not making a test flight.'

'But, well, that is, suppose something goes wrong?'

'Den de spacesuit keeps me alive for several hours and you can stand vacuum about de same lengt' of time. Emily vill be vatching us t'rough de ships's telescope, so she can let McConnell out and he can come rescue us.'

'And what if he can't find us? Or if we have an accident out of telescopic range from here? Space is a large volume.'

'I prefer you vould not mention dat possibility,' said Herr Syrup with a touch of hauteur.

Sarmishkidu shuddered. 'The things that an honest businessman has got to – *Donnervetter! Was ist das?*'

The sharp crack was followed by an earthquake tremble

through girders and plates. Herr Syrup sat down, hard. The deck twitched beneath him. He bounced up and pelted toward the exit. 'Dat vas from de stern!' he shouted.

He whipped through the bulkhead door, Sarmishkidu toiling in his wake, and up an interhold ladder to the axial passageway. Emily Croft had just emerged from the galley, a frying pan in one hand and an apron tied around her classic peplum. 'Oh, dear,' she cried, 'I'm sure Rory's cake has fallen. What was that noise?'

'Yust vat I vould like to know.' The engineer flung himself down the corridor. As he neared the stern, a faint acrid whiff touched his nose. 'In de engine room, I am afraid,' he panted.

'The engine – *Rory!*' shrieked the girl.

'Comin', macushla,' said a cheerful voice, and the gigantic red-thatched shape swung itself up from the after companionway.

Rory McConnell hooked thumbs in his belt, planted his booted feet wide, and grinned all over his smoke-blackened snub face. Herr Syrup crashed to a halt and stared frog-eyed. The Erseman's green tunic hung in rags and blood trickled from his nose. But the soot only made his teeth the more wolfishly white and his eyes the more high-voltage blue, while his bare torso turned out to carry even thicker muscles than expected.

'Well, well, well,' he beamed. 'An' so here we all are ag'in. Emily, me love, I ask your humble pardon for inny damage, but I couldn't wait longer for the sight of yez.'

'Vat have you done?' wailed Herr Syrup.

'Oh, well, sir, 'twas nothin'. I had me cartridges, an' a can opener an' me teeth an' other such tools. So I extracted the powder, tamped it in an auld beer bottle, lay a fuse, fired me last shot to light same, an' blew out one of them doors. An' now, sir, let's have a look at what ye been doin' this past week, an' then I think it best we return to the cool green hills of Grendel.'

'Ooooh,' said Herr Syrup.

McConnell laughed so that the hall rang with his joy, looked into the stricken wide gaze of his beloved and opened his arms. 'No so much as a kiss to seal the betrothal?' he said.

'Oh . . . yes . . . I'm sorry, darling.' Emily ran toward him.

'I *am* sorry,' she choked, burst into tears, and clanged the frying pan down on his head.

McConnell staggered, tripped on his boots, recovered, and waltzed in a circle. 'Get away!' screamed Emily. 'Get away!'

Herr Syrup paused for one frozen instant. Then he flung out a curse, whirled, and pounded back along the corridor. At the interhold ladderhead he found Sarmishkidu, puffing along at the slow pace of a Martian under Terrestrial gee. 'What has transpired?' asked Sarmishkidu.

Herr Syrup scooped him up under one arm and bounded down the ladder. 'Hey!' squealed the Martian. 'Let me go! *Bist du ganz geistegestört?* What do you mean, sir? *Urush nergatar shalmu ishkadan!* This instant! *Versteh'st du?*'

Rory McConnell staggered to the nearest wall and leaned on it for a few seconds. His eyes cleared. With a hoarse growl he sprang after the engineer. Emily stuck a shapely leg in his path. Down he went.

'Please!' she wept. 'Please, darling, don't make me do this!'

'They're gettin' away!' bawled McConnell. He got to his feet. Emily hit him with the frying pan. He sagged back to hands and knees. She stooped over him, frantically, and kissed the battered side of his head. He lurched erect. Emily slugged him again.

'You're being cruel' she sobbed.

The bulkhead door closed behind Herr Syrup. He set the

unloading controls. 'Ve ban getting out of here,' he panted. 'Before de Erser gets to de master svitch and stops every-t'ing cold.'

'What Erser?' sputtered Sarmishkidu indignantly.

'Ours.' Herr Syrup trotted toward the beer boat.

'Oh, that one!' Sarmishkidu hurried after him.

Herr Syrup climbed to the top of his boat's hull and lifted the space armor torso. Sarmishkidu swarmed after him like a herpetarium gone mad. The Dane dropped the Martian inside, took a final checkaround, and lowered himself. He screwed the spacesuit into place and hunched, breathing heavily. His bicycle headlamp was the only illumination in the box. It showed him the bicycle itself, braced upright with the little generator hitched to its rear wheel; the pants of his space armor, seated on a case of beer; a bundle of navigation instruments, tables, pencils, slide rule, and note pad; a tool box; two oxygen cylinders and a CO_2-H_2O absorber unit with an electric blower, which would also circulate the air as needed during free fall; the haywired control levers which were supposed to steer the boat; Sarmishkidu, draped on a box of pretzels; and Claus, disdainfully stealing from a box of popcorn which Herr Syrup suddenly realized he had no way of popping. And then, of course, himself.

It was rather cramped quarters.

The air pump roared, evacuating the chamber. Herr Syrup saw darkness thicken outside the boat windows, as the fluoro light ceased to be diffused. And then the great hatch swung ponderously open, and steel framed a blinding circle of stars.

'Hang on!' he yelled. 'Here ve go!'

The derrick scanned the little boat with beady photo-electric eyes, seized it in four claws, lifted it, and pitched it delicately through the hatch, which thereupon closed with an air of good riddance to bad rubbish. Since there was no machine outside to receive the boat, it turned end for end, spun a few meters from the *Mercury Girl*, and drifted along in much the same orbit, still trying to rotate on three simultaneous axes.

Herr Syrup gulped. The transition to weightlessness was an outrage, and the stars ramping around his field of view didn't help matters. His stomach lurched. Sarmishkidu groaned, hung onto the pretzel box with all six tentacles, and covered his eyes with his ears. Claus screamed, turning end for end in midair, and tried without success to fly. Herr Syrup reached for a control lever but didn't quite make it. Sarmishkidu uncovered one sick eye long enough to mumble: 'Bloody blank blasted Coriolis force.' Herr Syrup clenched his teeth, caught a mouthful of mustache, grimaced, spat it out, and tried again. This time he laid hands on the switch and pulled.

A cloud of beer gushed frostily from one of the transverse pipes. After several rather unfortunate attempts, Herr Syrup managed to stop the boat's rotation. He looked around him. He hung in darkness, among blazing stars. Grendel was a huge gibbous green moon to starboard. The *Mercury Girl* was a long rusty spindle to port. The asteroid sun, small and weak but perceived by the adaptable human eye as quite bright enough, poured in through the spacesuit helmet in the roof and bounced dazzlingly off his bare scalp.

He swallowed sternly, to remind his stomach who was boss, and began taking navigational sights. Sarmishkidu rolled a red look 'upward' at Claus, who clung miserably to the Martian's head with eyes tightly shut.

Herr Syrup completed his figuring. It would have been best to wait a while yet, to get the maximum benefit of orbital velocity toward New Winchester; but McConnell was not going to wait. Anyhow, this was such a slow orbit that it didn't make much difference. Most likely the factor would be quite lost among the fantastically uncertain quantities of the boat itself. One would have to take what the good Lord sent. He gripped the control levers.

A low murmur filled the cabin as the rearmost beer barrel snorted its vapors into space. There was a faint backward tug of acceleration pressure, which mounted very gradually as mass decreased. The thrust was not centered with absolute precision, and of course the distribution of mass throughout the whole structure was hit-or-miss, so the boat began to pick up a spin again. Steering by the seat of his pants and a few primitive meters, Herr Syrup corrected that tendency with side jets.

Blowing white beer fumes in all directions, the messenger boat moved slowly along a wobbling spiral toward New Winchester.

CHAPTER TEN

'Oh darling, dearest, beloved,' wept Emily, dabbing at Rory McConnell's head, 'forgive me!'

'I love yez too,' said the Erseman, sitting up, 'but unliss ye'll stop poundin' in me skull I'll have to lock yez up for the duration.'

'I promise . . . I promise . . . oh, I couldn't bear it! Sweetheart—' Emily clutched his arm as he rose – 'can't you let them go now? I mean, they've gotten clean away, you've lost, so why don't we wait here and, well, I mean to say, really.'

'What do you mean to say?'

Emily blushed and lowered her eyes. 'If you don't know,' she said in a prim voice, 'I shall certainly not tell you.'

McConnell blushed too.

Then, resolutely, he started toward the bridge. The girl hurried after him. He flung back: 'Tell me what it is they're escapin' in, an' maybe I'll be ready to concede hon'rable defeat.' But having been informed, he only barked a laugh and said, 'Well, an' 'tis a gallant try, 'tis, but me with a regular spaceship at me beck can't admit the end of the game. In fact, me dear, I'm sorry to say they haven't a Plutonian's chance in hell.'

By that time he was in the turret, sweeping the skies with its telescope. It took him a while to find the boat, already it was a mere speck in the gleaming dark. He scowled, chewed his lip, and muttered half to himself:

' 'Twill take time to extract the polarity reverser, an' me not a trained engineer. By then the craft will be indeed hard to locate. If I went on down to Grendel to get help, 'twould take hours to reach the ear of himself an' assimble a crew, if I know me Erse lads. An' hours is too long. So – I'll have to go after our friends there alone. Acushla, I don't think ye'll betray their cause if ye fix me a sandwich or six an' open me a bottle of beer whilst I work.'

McConnell did, in fact, require almost an hour to get the geegee repulsors to repulsing again. With the compensator still on the fritz, that put the ship's interior back in free fall state. He floated, dashing the sweat from his brow, and smiled at Emily. 'Go strap yourself in, me rose of Grendel, for I may well have to make some sharp maneuvers an' I wouldn't be bruisin' of that fair skin – Damn! Git away!' That was addressed to the sweat he had just dashed from his brow. Swatting blindly at the fog of tiny globules, he pushed one leg against a wall and arrowed out the door.

Up in the turret again, harnessed in his seat before the pilot console, he tickled its control and heard the engines purr. 'Are ye ready, darlin'?' he called into the intercom.

'Not yet, sweetheart,' Emily's voice floated back. 'One moment, please.'

'A moment only,' warned McConnell, squinting into the telescope. He could not have found the fleeing boat at all were it not for the temporary condensation of beer vapor into a cloud as expansion chilled it. And all he saw was a tiny, ghostly nebula on the very edge of vision. To be sure, knowing approximately what path the fugitives must follow gave him a track; he could doubtless always come within a hundred kilometers of them that way; but—

'Are ye ready, me sugar?'

'Not yet, love. I'll be with you in a jiffy.'

McConnell drummed impatient fingers on the console. The *Mercury Girl* swung gently around Grendel. His head still throbbed.

'Da-a-arlin'! Time's a-wastin'! We'll be late!'

'Oh, give me just a sec. Really, dearest, you might remember when we're married and have to go out someplace a girl wants to look her best, and that takes time, I mean dresses and cosmetics and so on aren't classical but I guess if I can give up my principles for you so you can be proud of me and if I can eat the things you like even if they aren't natural, well, then you can wait a little while for me to make myself presentable and—'

'A man has two choices in this universe,' said McConnell grimly to himself, 'he can remain celibate or he can resign himself to spendin' ten per cent of his life waitin' for women.'

He glared at the chronometer. 'We're late already!' he snapped. 'I'll have to run off a different approach curve to our orbit an'—'

'Well, you can be doing it, can't you? I mean, instead of just sitting there grumbling at me, why don't you do something constructive like punching that old computer or whatever it is?'

McConnell stiffened. 'Emily,' he said through thinned lips, 'are ye by any chance stallin' me?'

'Why, Rory, how could you? Merely because a girl has to—'

He calculated the required locus and said, 'Ye've got just sixty seconds to prepare for acceleration.'

'But Rory!'

'Fifty seconds.'

'But I mean to say, actually—'

'Forty seconds.'

'Oh, right-o, then. And I'm not angry with you, love, really I'm not. I mean, I want you to know a girl admires a man like you who actually is a man. Why, what would I do with one of those awful "Yes, dear" types, they're positively Roman! Imperial Roman, I mean. The Republican Romans were at least virile, though of course they were barbarians and rather hairy. But what I meant to say, Rory, is that one reason I love you so much—'

After about five minutes of this, Major McConnell realized what was going on. With an inarticulate snarl he stabbed the computer, corrected his curve for time lost, punched it into the autopilot, and slapped down the main drive switch.

First the ship turned, seeking her direction, and then a Terrestrial gravity of acceleration pushed him back into the chair. No reason to apply more; he felt sure that leprechaun job he was chasing could scarcely pick up one meter per second squared, and matching velocities would be a tricky enough business for one man alone. He saw Grendel swing past the starboard viewport and drop behind. He applied a repulsor field forward to kill some of his present speed, simultaneously giving the ship an impulse toward ten-thirty o'clock, twenty-three degrees 'high'. In a smooth arc, the *Mercury Girl* picked up the trail of Herr Syrup and began to close the gap.

'Ah, now we'll end this tale,' murmured Rory McConnell, 'an' faith, ye've been a worthy foeman an 'tis not I that will stint ye when we meet ag'in in some friendly pub after the glorious redemption of Gaelic La – Oops!'

For a horrible moment, he thought that some practical joker had pulled the seat out from under him. He fell toward the floor, tensing his gluteal muscles for the crash . . . and fell, and fell, and after a few seconds realized he was in free fall.

'What the jumpin' blue hell?' he roared and glared at the

control board meters, just as the lights went out.

A thousand stars leered through the viewport. McConnell clawed blindly at his harness. He heard the ventilator fans sigh to a halt. The stillness became frightful. 'Emily!' he shouted, 'Emily, where are ye?' There was no reply. Somehow he found the intercom switch and jiggled it. Only a mechanical clicking answered; that circuit was also dead.

Groping and flailing his way aft, he needed black minutes to reach the engine room. It was like a cave. He entered, blind, drifting free, fanning the air with one invisible hand to keep from smothering in his own unventilated exhalations, his heartbeat thick and horrible in his ears. There should be a flashlight clipped somewhere near the door – but where? 'Mother of God!' he groaned. 'Are we fallen into the devil's fingers?'

A small sound came from somewhere in the gloom. 'What's that?' he bawled. 'Who's there? Where are ye? Speak up before I beat the bejasus out of yez, ye—' and he went on with a richness of description to be expected when Gaelic blood has had a checkered career.

'Rory!' said an offended feminine voice out of the abyss. 'If you are going to use that kind of language before me, you can just wipe your mouth out and not come back until you are prepared to say it in Greek like a gentleman! I mean, really!'

'Are ye here? Darlin', are ye here? I thought—'

'Well,' said the girl, 'I know I promised not to hit you any more, and I wouldn't, not for all the world, but I still have to do what I can, don't I, dear? I mean, if I gave up you'd just despise me. It wouldn't be British.'

'*What have ye done?*'

After a long pause, Emily said in a small voice: 'I don't know.'

'How's that?' snapped McConnell.

'I just went over to that control panel or whatever it is and started pulling switches. I mean to say, you don't expect me to know what all those things are for, do you? Because I don't. However,' said Emily brightly, 'I can parse Greek verbs.'

'Oh . . . no!' groaned McConnell. He began fumbling his way toward the invisible board. Where was it, anyhow?

'I can cook too,' said Emily. 'And sew. And I'm awfully fond of children.'

Herr Syrup noted on his crude meters that the first-stage beer barrel was now exhausted. He pulled the switch that dropped it and pushed himself up into the spacesuit to make sure that that had actually been done. Peering through the helmet globe, he saw that one relay had stuck and the keg still clung. He popped back inside and told Sarmishkidu to hand him some sections of iron pipe through the stovepipe valve; this emergency was not unanticipated. Clumsy in gauntlets, his fingers screwed the pieces together to make a prod which could reach far aft and crack the empty cask loose.

It occurred to him how much simpler it would have been to keep his tools in a box fastened to the outer hull. But of course such things only come to mind when a model is being tested.

He stared aft. The *Mercury Girl* was visible to the unaided eye, though dwindling perceptibly. She still floated inert, but he could not expect that condition to prevail for long. Well, a man can but try. Herr Syrup wriggled out of the armor torso and back into the cabin. Claus was practicing free-fall flight technique and nipping stray droplets of beer out of the air; sometimes he collided with a drifting empty bottle, but he seemed to enjoy himself.

'Resuming acceleration,' said Herr Syrup. 'Give me a pretzel.'

Suds gushed from the second barrel. The boat wobbled crazily. Of course the loss of the first one had changed its spin characteristics. Herr Syrup compensated and ploughed doggedly on. The second cask emptied and was discharged without trouble. He cut in the third one.

Presently Sarmishkidu crawled 'up' into the spacesuit. A whistle escaped him.

'Vat?' asked Herr Syrup.

'There – behind us – your spaceship – und it is coming *verdammten* fast!'

Having strapped his fiancée carefully into the acceleration chair beside his own, Rory McConnell resumed pursuit. He had lost a couple of hours by now, between one thing and another. And while she drifted free, the *Girl* had of course orbited well off the correct track. He had to get back on it and then start casting about. For a half hour of strained silence, he maneuvered.

'There!' he said at last.

'Where?' asked Emily.

'In the 'scope,' said McConnell. His ill humor let up and he squeezed her hand. 'Hang on, here we go. I'll have thim back aboard in ten minutes.'

The hazy cloud waxed so fast that he revised his estimate upward. He had too much velocity; it would be necessary to overshoot, brake, and come back—

Then *crash! clang-ng-ng!* His teeth jarred together. For a moment, his heart paused and he knew naked fear.

'What was that?' asked Emily.

He hated to frighten her, but he forced out of suddenly

stiff and sandy lips: 'A meteor, I'm sure. An' judging from the sound of it, 'twas big an' fast enough to stave in a whole compartment.' You could not exactly roll your eyes heavenward in free space, but he tried manfully. 'Holy St. Patrick, is this any way to treat your loyal son?'

He shot past the wallowing beer boat at kilometers per second, falling free while he ripped off his harness. 'The instruments aren't showin' damage, but belike the crucial one is been knocked out,' he muttered. 'An' us with no engine crew an' no deckhands. I'll have to go out there meself to check. At least this section is unharmed.' He nodded at the handkerchief he had thrown into the air; when the ventilators were briefly turned off, it simply hung, borne on no current of leakage. 'If we begin to lose air elsewhere, sweetheart, there'll be automatic ports to seal yez off, so ye're all right for the next few hours.'

'But what about you?' she cried, white-faced now that she understood. 'What about you?'

'I'll be in a spacesuit.' He leaned over and kissed her. ' 'Tis not the danger that's so great as the delay. For somethin' I'll have to do, jist so acceleration strain don't pull the damaged hull apart. I'll be back when I can, darlin'.'

And yet, as he went aft, there was no sealing bulwark in his way, nowhere a wind whistling toward the dread emptiness outside. Puzzled and more than a little daunted, Rory McConnell completed his interior inspection in the engine room, broke out his own outsize space armor from his pack, and donned it: a slow, awkward task for one man alone. He floated to the nearest airlock and let himself out.

It was eerie on the hull, where only his clinging bootsoles held him fast among streaming cold constellations. The harshness of undiffused sunlight and the absolute blackness of shadow made it hard to recognize anything for what it was.

He saw a goblin and crossed himself violently before realizing it was only a lifeboat tank; and he was an experienced spaceman.

An hour's search revealed no leak. There was a dent in the bow which might or might not be freshly made, nothing else. And yet that meteor had struck with such a doomsday clang that he had thought the hull might be torn in two. Well, evidently St. Patrick had been on the job. McConnell returned inside, disencumbered himself, went forward, reassured Emily, and began to kill his unwanted velocity.

Almost two hours had passed before he was back in the vicinity of the accident, and then he could not locate the fugitive boat. By now it would have ceased blasting; darkly painted, it would be close to invisible in this black sky. He would have to set up a search pattern and – He groaned.

Something drifted across his telescopic field of view. What the deuce? He nudged the spaceship closer, and gasped.

'Son of a—' Hastily, he switched to Gaelic.

'What is it, light of both my eyes?' asked Emily.

McConnell beat his head against the console. 'A couple of hoops an' some broken staves,' he whimpered. 'Oh, no, no, no!'

'But what of it? I mean, after all, when you consider how Mr. Syrup put that boat together, well, actually.'

'That's just it!' howled McConnell. 'That's what's cost me near heart failure, plus two priceless hours or more an'— That was our meteor! An empty beer barrel! Oh, the ignominy of it!'

CHAPTER ELEVEN

Herr Syrup stopped the exhaust of his fourth-stage keg and leaned back into weightlessness with a sigh. 'Ve better not accelerate any more,' he said. 'Not yust now. Ve vill need a little reserve to maneuver later on.'

'Vot later on?' asked Herr von Himmelschmidt sourly. 'I don't know vy der ship shot on past us, but soon it comes back und den ve iss maneuvered into chail.'

'Vell, meanvile shall ve pass de time?' Herr Syrup took a greasy pack of cards from his jacket and riffled them suggestively.

'Stop riffling them suggestively!' squealed Sarmishkidu. 'This is no time for idle amusements.'

'Well . . . hmmm . . . no, not that . . . Perhaps . . . no . . . Shilling ante?'

At the end of some four hours, when he was ahead by several pounds sterling in I.O.U.'s and Sarmishkidu was whistling like an indignant bagpipe, Herr Syrup noticed how dim the light was getting. The gauge showed him that the outside batteries were rather run down also. Everything would have to be charged up again. He explained the situation. 'Do you vant first turn on de bicycle or shall I?' he asked.

'Who, me?' Sarmishkidu wagged a languid ear. 'Whatever gave you the idea that evolution has prepared my race for bicycle riding?'

'Vell . . . I mean . . . dat is—'

'You are letting your Danishness run away with you.'

'*Satan i helvede!*' muttered Herr Syrup. He floated himself into the saddle, put feet to pedals, and began working.

'And de vorst of it is,' he grumbled, 'who is ever going to believe I crossed from Grendel to New Vinshester on a bicycle?'

Slowly, majestically, and off-center, the boat picked up an opposite rotation.

'There they be!' cried Rory McConnell.

'Oh dear,' said Emily Croft.

The beer boat swelled rapidly in the forward viewport. The weariness of hour upon hour, searching, dropped from the Erseman. 'Here we go!' he cried exultantly. '*Tantivy, tantivy, tantivy!*'

Then, lacking radar, he found that the human eye is a poor judge of free-space relationships. He buckled down to the awkward task of matching speeds.

'Whoops!' he said. 'Overshot!' Ten kilometers beyond, he came to a relative halt, twisted the cumbersome mass of the ship around, and approached slowly. He saw a head pop up into the spacesuit helmet, glare at him, and pop back again. Foam spouted; the boat slipped out of his view.

McConnell readjusted and came alongside, so that he looked directly from the turret at his prey. 'He hasn't the acceleration to escape us,' he gloated. 'I'll folly each twist an' turn he cares to make, from now until—' He stopped.

'Until we get to New Winchester?' asked Emily in a demure tone.

'But – I mean to say – but!' Major McConnell bugged tired eyes at the keg-and-box bobbing across the stars.

'But I've overhauled them!' he shouted, pounding the console. 'I've a regular ship with hundreds of times their mass an'...an'...they've got to come aboard! It isn't fair!'

'Since we have no wireless, how can you inform them of that?' purred the girl. She leaned over close and patted his cheek. Her gaze softened. 'There, there. I'm sorry. I do love you, and I don't want to tease you or anything, but honestly, don't you think you're becoming a bit of a bore on this subject? I mean, enough's enough, don't you know.'

'Not if ye're of Erse blood, it isn't.' McConnell set his jaw till it ached. 'I'll scoop 'em up, that's what I will!'

There was a master control for the cargo machinery in the engine room, but none on the bridge. McConnell unstrapped himself, shoved grimly 'down' to the hold section, pumped out the main hatch chamber and opened the lock. Now he had it gaping wide enough to swallow the boat whole, and—

Weight came back. He crashed into the deck. 'Emily!' he bellowed, picking himself up with a bloody nose. 'Emily, git away from them controls!'

Three Terrestrial gravities of acceleration were a monstrous load on any man. He took minutes to regain the bridge, drag himself to the main console, and slap down the main drive switch. Meanwhile Emily, sagging in her chair and gasping for breath, managed a tolerant smile.

When they again floated free, McConnell bawled at her: 'I love yez more than I do me own soul, an' ye're the most beautiful creature the cosmos will ever see, an' I've half a mind to turn yez over me knee an' paddle ye raw!'

'Watch your language, Rory,' the vicar's daughter reproved. 'Paddle me black and blue, *if* you please. I mean, I don't like *double-entendres*.'

'Ah, be still, ye blitherin' angel,' he snarled. He swept the sky with a bloodshot telescope. The boat was out of sight again. Of course.

It took him half an hour to relocate it, still orbiting stubbornly on toward New Winchester. And New Winchester had grown noticeably more bright.

'Now we'll see what we'll see,' grated Major McConnell.

He accelerated till he was dead ahead of the boat, matched speeds – except for a few K.P.H. net toward him which he left for his quarry – and spun broadside to. As nearly as he could gauge it, the boat was aimed directly into his open cargo hatch.

Herr Syrup applied a quick side jet, slipped 'beneath' the larger hull, and continued on his way.

'*Aaaargh!*' Tiny flecks of foam touched McConnell's lips. He tried again.

And again.

And again.

'It's no use,' he choked at last. 'He can slide past me too easy. The wan thing I could do would be to ram him an' be done – Arragh, hell have him, he knows I'm not a murderer.'

'Really, dear,' said Emily, 'it would all be so simple if you would just give up and admit he's won.'

'Small chance of that!' McConnell brooded for a long minute. And slowly a luster returned to his eyes. 'Yes. I have it. The loadin' crane. I'll have to jury-rig a control to the bridge, as well as a visio screen so I can see what I'm doin'. But havin' given meself that much, why, I'll approach ag'in with the crane grapple projectin' from the hatch, reach out, an' grab hold!'

'Rory,' said Emily, 'you're being tiresome.'

'I'm bein' Erse, by all the saints!' McConnell rubbed a bristly red jaw. ' 'Tis hours 'twill take me, an' him fleein' the while. Could ye hold us alongside, me only one?'

'Me?' The girl opened wide blue eyes and protested innocently. 'But darling, you told me after that last time to leave the controls alone, and I admit I don't know a thing about it.

I mean, it would be unlawful for me to try piloting, wouldn't it, and positively dangerous. I mean to say, *medén pratto.*'

'Ah, well, I might have known how the good loyal heart of yez would make ye a bloody nuisance. But either give me your word of honor not to touch the pilot board ag'in, or I must break me own heart by tyin' yez into that chair.'

'Oh, I promise, dear. I'll promise you anything within reason.'

'An' whatsoever ye don't happen to want is unreasonable. Yes.' Rory McConnell sighed, kissed his lady love, and went off to work. The escape boat blasted feebly but steadily into a new orbit – not very different, but time and the pull of the remote sun on an inert ship would show their work later on.

General Scourge-of-the-Sassenach O'Toole lifted a gaunt face and glared somberly at the young guardsman who had finally won through to his office. 'Well?' he clipped.

'Beggin' your pardon, sir, but—'

'Salute me, ye good-for-nothin' scut!' growled O'Toole. 'What kind of an army is it we've got here, where a private soldier passin' the captain in the street slaps his back an' says, "Paddy, ye auld pig, the top of the mornin' to yez an' if ye've a moment to spare, why, 'tis proud I'll be to stand yez a mug of dark in yon tavern" – eh?'

'Well, sir,' said the guardsman, his Celtic love of disputation coming to the fore, 'I say 'twas a fine well-run army of outstandingly high morale. Though truth to speak, the captain I've been saddled with is a pickle-faced son of a landlord who would not lift his hat to St. Bridget herself, did the dear holy colleen come walkin' in his door.'

'Morale, ye say?' shouted O'Toole, springing from his chair. 'Morale cuts both ways, ye idiot! How much morale do ye think the officer's corps has got, or I meself, when me own men name me Auld S.O.T.S. to me face, not even bother-in' to sound the initials sep'rit, an' me havin' not touched a drop in all me life? I'll have some respect hereabouts, be-gorra, or know the reason why!'

'If ye want to know the reason I can give it to ye, General, sir, ye auld maid in britches!' cried the guardsman. His fist smote the desk. ' 'Tis just the sour face of yez, that's the rayson, an' if ye drink no drop 'tis because wan look at yez would curdle the poteen in the jug! Now if ye want some constructive suggestions for improvin' the management of this army—'

They passed an enjoyable half hour. At last, having grown hoarse, the guardsman bade the general a friendly good day and departed.

Five minutes later there was a scuffle in the anteroom. A sentry's voice yelped, 'Ye can't go in there to himself with-out an appointment!' and the guardsman answered, 'An ap-pointment I've had, since the hour before dawn whin I first came an' tried to get by the bureaucratic lot of yez!' and the scuffle got noisier and at last the office door went off its hinges as the guardsman tossed the sentry through it.

'Beggin' your pardon, sir,' he panted, dabbing at a bruised cheek and judiciously holding the sentry down with one booted foot, 'but I just remembered why I had to see yez.'

'Ye'll go to the brig for this, ye riotous scum!' roared O'Toole. 'Corp'ril of the guard! Arrest this man!'

'That attitude is precisely what I was criticizin' earlier,' pointed out the soldier. ' 'Tis officers like yez what takes all the fun out of war. Why, ye wall-eyed auld Fomorian, if ye'd been in charge of the Cattle Raid of Cooley, the Brown Bull would still be chewin' cud in his meaddy! Now ye listen to me—'

As four freshly arrived sentries dragged him off, he shouted back: 'All right, then! If ye're goin' to be that way about it, all right an' be damned to yez! I won't tell ye my news! I won't speak a word of what I saw through the tellyscope just before sunrise – or failed to see – ye can sit there in blithe ignorance of the Venusian ship havin' vanished from her orbit, till she calls down the Anglian Navy upon yez! See if I care!'

For a long, long moment, General Scourge-of-the-Sassenach O'Toole gaped out at Grendel's blue sky.

CHAPTER TWELVE

Spent, shaking with lack of sleep and sheer muscular weariness, Rory McConnell weaved through free fall toward the bridge. As he passed the galley, Emily stopped him. Having had a night watch of rest, she looked almost irritatingly calm and beautiful. 'There, there, love,' she said. 'Is it all over with? Come, I've fixed a nice cup of tea.'

'Don't want any tea,' he growled.

'Oh, but darling, you must! Why, you'll waste away. I swear you're already just skin and bones . . . oh, and your poor dear hands, the knuckles are all rubbed raw. Come on, there's a sweetheart, sit down and have a cup of tea. I mean, actually you'll have to float, and drink it out of one of those silly suction bottles, but the principle is the same. That old boat will keep.'

'Not much longer,' said McConnell. 'By now, she's far closer to the King than she is to Grendel.'

'But you can wait ten minutes, can't you?' Emily pouted. 'You're not only neglecting your health, but me. You've hardly remembered I exist. All those hours, the only thing I heard on the intercom was swearing. I mean, I imagine from the tone it was swearing, though of course I don't speak Gaelic. You will have to teach me after we're married. And I'll teach you Greek. I understand there is a certain affinity between the languages.' She rubbed her cheek against his bare chest. 'Just as there is between you and me . . . Oh, dear!' She retired to try getting some of the engine grease off her face.

In the end, Rory McConnell did allow himself to be prevailed upon. For ten minutes only. Half an hour later, much refreshed, he mounted to the bridge and resumed acceleration.

Grendel was little more than a tarnished farthing among the stars. New Winchester had swelled until it was a great green and gold moon. There would be warships in orbit around it, patrolling – McConnell dismissed the thought and gave himself to his search.

After all this time, it was not easy. Space is big and even the largest beer keg is comparatively small. Since Herr Syrup had shifted the plane of his boat's orbit by a trifle – an hour's questing confirmed that this must be the case – the volume in which he might be was fantastically huge. Furthermore, drifting free, his vessel painted black, he would be hard to spot, even when you were almost on top of him.

Another hour passed.

'Poor darling,' said Emily, reaching from her chair to rumple the major's red locks. 'You've tried so hard.'

New Winchester continued to grow. Its towns were visible now, as blurred specks on a subtle tapestry of wood and field and ripening grain; the Royal Highroad was a thin streak across a cloud-softened dayface.

'He'll have to reveal himself soon,' muttered McConnell from his telescope. 'That beer blast is so weak—'

'Dear me, I understood Mr. Sarmishkidu's beer was rather strong,' said Emily.

McConnell chuckled. 'Ah, they should have used Irish whisky in their jet. But what I meant, me beloved, was that in so cranky a boat, they could not hope to hit their target on the nose, so they must make course corrections as they approach it. And with so low an exhaust velocity, they'll need a long time of blastin' to – *Hoy! I've got him!*'

The misty trail expanded in the viewfield, far and far away. McConnell's hands danced on the control board. The spaceship turned about and leaped ahead. The crane, projecting out of the cargo hatch, flexed its talons hungrily.

Fire burst!

After a time of strangling on his own breath, McConnell saw the brightness break into rags before his dazzled eyes. He stared into night and constellations. 'What the devil?' he gasped. 'Is there a Sassenach ship nearby? Has the auld squarehead a gun? That was a shot across our bows!'

He zipped past the boat at a few kilometers' distance while frantically scouring the sky. A massive shape crossed his telescopic field. It grew before his eyes as he stared – it couldn't be— 'Our own ship!' choked McConnell. 'Our own Erse ship.'

The converted freighter did not shoot again, for fear of attracting Anglian attention. It edged nearer, awkwardly seeking to match velocities and close in on the *Mercury Girl*. 'Get away!' shouted McConnell. 'Get out of the way, ye idiots! 'Tis not meself ye want, 'tis auld Syrup, over there. Git out of me way!' He avoided imminent collision by a wild backward spurt.

The realization broke on him. 'But how do they know 'tis me on board here?' he asked aloud.

'Telepathy!' suggested the girl, fluttering her lashes at him.

'They don't know. They can't even have noticed the keg boat, I'll swear. So 'tis us they wish to board an' – Get out of the way, ye son of a Scotchman!'

The Erse ship rushed in, shark-like. Again McConnell had to accelerate backward to avoid being stove. New Winchester dwindled in his viewports.

He slapped the console with a furious hand. 'An' me lackin' a radio to tell 'em the truth,' he groaned. 'I'll jist have to orbit free, an' let 'em lay alongside an' board, an' explain the situation.' His teeth grated together. 'All of which, if I know any one thing about the Force's high command, will cost us easy another hour.'

Emily smiled. The *Mercury Girl* continued to recede from the goal.

'I t'ink ve is in good broadcast range now,' said Herr Syrup.

His boat was again inert, having exhausted nearly all its final cask. New Winchester waxed, already spreading across several degrees of arc. If only some circling Navy ship would happen to see the vessel; but no, the odds were all against that. Ah, well. Weary, bleary, but justifiably triumphant, Herr Syrup tapped the oscillator key.

Nothing happened.

'Vere's de spark?' he complained.

'I don't know,' said Sarmishkidu. 'I thought you would.'

'Bloody hell!' screamed Claus.

Herr Syrup snarled inarticulately and tapped some more. There was still no result. 'It was okay ven I tested back at de ship,' he pleaded. 'Of course, I did not dare test much or de Ersers might overhear, but it did vork. Vat's gone crazy since?'

'I vould suggest that since most of the transmission apparatus is outside by the batteries, something has worked loose,' answered Sarmishkidu. 'We could easily have jarred a wire off its terminal or some such thing.'

Herr Syrup swore and stuffed himself up into the spacesuit and tried to see what was wrong. But the oscillator parts were not accessible, or even visible, from this position: another point overlooked in the haste of constructing the boat. So he would have to put on the complete suit and crawl back to attempt repairs; and that would expose the interior of the cabin, including poor old Claus, to raw space – 'Oh, Yudas,' he said.

There was no possibility of landing on New Winchester; there never had been, in fact. Now the barrel didn't even hold enough reaction mass to establish an orbit. The boat would drift by, the oxygen would be exhausted, unless first the enemy picked him up. Staring aft, Herr Syrup gulped. The enemy was about to do so.

He had grinned when he saw the Erse-controlled ships nudge each other out of sight. But now one of them, yes, the *Girl* herself, with a grapnel out at the side, came back into view.

His heart sagged. Well, he had striven. He might as well give up. Life in a yeast factory was at least life.

No, by heaven!

Herr Syrup struggled back into the box. 'Qvick!' he yelled. 'Give me de popcorn!'

'What?' gaped Sarmishkidu.

'Hand me up de carton vit' popcorn t'rough the valve, an' den give me about a minute of full acceleration forvard.'

Sarmishkidu shrugged with all his tentacles, but obeyed. A quick pair of blasts faced the boat away from the approaching ship. Herr Syrup's space-gauntleted hand closed on the small box as it was shoved up through the stovepipe diaphragm, and he hurled it from him as his vessel leaped ahead.

The popcorn departed with a speed which, relative to the *Girl*, was not inconsiderable. Exposed to vacuum, it exploded from its pasteboard container as it gained full, puffy dimensions.

Now one of the oldest space war tactics is to drop a mass of hard objects, such as ball bearings, in the path of a pursuing enemy. And then there are natural meteors. In either case, the speeds involved are often such as to wreak fearful damage on the craft. Rory McConnell saw a sudden ghastly vision of white spheroids hurtling toward him. Instinctively, he stopped forward acceleration and crammed on full thrust sideways.

Almost, he dodged the swarm. A few pieces did strike the viewport. But they did not punch through, they did not even crater the tough plastic. They spattered. It took him several disgusted minutes to realize what they had been. By that time, the Erse ship had come into view with the plain intention of stopping him, laying alongside, and finding out what the devil was wrong now. When everything had been straightened out, a good half hour had passed.

'Dere is for damn sure no time to fix de oscillator,' said Herr Syrup. 'Ve must do vat ve can.'

Sarmishkidu worked busily, painting the large pretzel box with air-sealing gunk. 'I trust the bird will survive,' he said.

'I t'ink so,' said Herr Syrup. 'I t'row him and de apparatus avay as hard as I can. Ve vill pass qvite close to de fringes of de asteriod's atmosphere. He has not many minutes to fall, and de oxygen keeps him breat'ing all dat vile. Ven de whole t'ing hits de air envelope, dere vill be enough impact to tear open de pretzel box and Claus can fly out.'

The boat rumbled softly, blasting as straight toward New Winchester as its crew had been able to aim. It gave a feeble but most useful weight to objects within. Sarmishkidu finished painting the box and attached a tube connecting it with one of the oxygen flasks.

'Now, den, Claus,' said Herr Syrup, 'I have tied a written

message to your leg, but if I know you, you vill rip it off and eat it as soon as you are free. However, if I also know you, you vill fly straight for de nearest pub and try to bum a beer. So, repeat after me: "Help! Help!! Invaders on Grendel." Dat's all. "Help! Help! Invaders on Grendel."'

'McConnell is a skunk,' said Claus.

'No, no! "Help! Invaders on Grendel."'

'McConnell cheats at cards,' said Claus. 'McConnell is a teetotaller. McConnell is a barnacle on de nose of society. McConnell—'

'No, no, no!'

'No, no, no!' echoed Claus agreeably.

'Listen,' said Herr Syrup after a deep breath. 'Listen, Claus. Please say it. Yust say, "Help! Help! Invaders on Grendel."'

'Nevermore,' said Claus.

'We had best proceed,' said Sarmishkidu.

He stuffed the indignant crow into the box and sealed it shut while Herr Syrup got back in the spacesuit: including, this time, its pants. And then, having aerated himself enough to stand vacuum for a while, Sarmishkidu unfastened the armor from the hatch cover. Herr Syrup popped inboard. Air rushed out. Herr Syrup pushed the oxygen cylinder, with Claus' box, through the hole.

New Winchester was so close it filled nearly half the sky. Herr Syrup made out towns and farms and orchards, through fleecy clouds. He sighed wistfully, shoved the tank from him as hard as he could, and watched it dwindle. A moment afterward, the asteroid itself began to recede; he had passed peri-New Winchester and was outward bound on a long cold orbit.

'So,' said Herr Syrup, 'let de Erse come pick us up.' He realized he was talking to himself: no radio, and anyhow

Sarmishkidu had curled into a ball. There was no point in resealing the cabin – the other oxygen bottle was long exhausted.

'I never t'ought de future of two nations could depend on vun old crow,' sighed Herr Syrup.

CHAPTER THIRTEEN

'Tsk-Tsk-Tsk,' said Rory McConnell. 'An' your radio didn't work after all?'

'No,' wheezed Herr Syrup. He was still a little blue around the nose. It had been a grim wait of many hours, crouched in the spinning wreckage of his boat; his suit's air supply had been low indeed when the *Mercury Girl* finally came to him.

'An' ye say your poor auld bird was lost as well?'

'Blown out ven de gasket blew out dat I told you of.' Herr Syrup accepted a cigar and leaned his weary frame gratefully back against the gymbal-swung acceleration bench in the saloon. There was still no functioning compensator and the *Mercury Girl*, with an Erse crew aboard, was pacing back to Grendel at a quarter gee.

'Then all your trouble was for nothin'?' McConnell did not gloat; if anything, he was too sympathetic.

'I guess so,' Herr Syrup answered rather bleakly, thinking of Claus. No doubt the crow would look at once for human society; but what was he likely to convey except a string of oaths? Too late, the engineer saw that he should have put some profanity into his message.

'Well, ye were a brave foe, an' 'tis daily I'll come by Grendel gaol to cheer yez,' said McConnell, clapping his shoulder. 'For I fear the General will insist on lockin' yez up for the duration. He was more than a little annoyed, I can tell yez;

he was spittin' rivets. He wanted for to leave you drift off to your fate, an' we had quite an argument about it, wherefore I am now just another private soldier in the ranks.' Mc-Connell rubbed his large knuckles reminiscently. 'However, I won me point. Himself went back hours ago in t'other ship, but he let me stay wi' this one and pick yez up. But I dared not go close to the Anglian capital, but must wait until ye had orbited so far away that no chance Navy ship would see us an' get curious. An' so long a delay meant ye were hard to find. We were almost too late, eh, what?'

'*Ja*,' shuddered Herr Syrup. He tilted the proffered bottle of Irish to his lips.

'But all's well that ends well, even though 'twas said by an Englishman,' chuckled McConnell. He squeezed Emily's hand. She smiled mistily back at him. 'For I'll regain me auld rank as soon as the swellin' in the General's eye has gone down so he can see how much I'm needed. An' then 'twill be time to effect the glorious redemption of Laoighise, an' then, Emily, you an' I will be wed, an' then – Well!' He coughed. She blushed.

'*Ja*,' snorted Sarmishkidu. 'Good ending, huh? With my business ruined, und me in jail, und maybe a war started, and that dummkopf of a *Shalmuannusar* claiming he proved the sub-unitary connectivity theorem before I did, as if publishing first had anything to do with priority – Ha!'

'Oh, dear,' said Emily compassionately.

'Oh, darlin',' said McConnell.

'Oh, sweetheart,' cooed Emily, losing interest in Sarmishkidu.

'Oh, me little turtle dove,' whispered McConnell.

Herr Syrup fought a strong desire to retch.

A bell clanged. McConnell stood up. 'That's the signal,' he said. 'We've come to Grendel an' I'll be wanted on the bridge. 'Twill be an unendin' few minutes till I see yez ag'in, me only one.'

'Goodbye, my beloved,' breathed the girl. Herr Syrup gritted his teeth.

Her manner changed as soon as the Erseman had left. She leaned over toward the engineer and asked tensely: 'Do you think we succeeded? I mean, do you?'

'I doubt it,' he sighed. 'In de end, only Claus vas left to carry de vord.' He explained what had happened. 'Even supposing he does repeat vat he vas supposed to, I doubt many people vould believe a crow dat has not even been introduced.'

'Well—' Emily bit her lip. 'We tried, didn't we? But if a war does come – between Rory's country and mine. No! I won't think about it!' She rubbed small fists across her eyes.

Uncompensated forces churned Herr Syrup on his seat. At last they quieted; the engine mumble died; a steady one gee informed him that the *Mercury Girl* was again berthed on Grendel. 'I'm going to Rory,' said Emily. Almost, she fled from the saloon.

Herr Syrup puffed his cigar, waiting for the Erse to come take him to prison. The first thing he would do there, he thought dully, was sleep for about fifty hours. . . . He grew aware that several minutes had passed. Sarmishkidu sat brooding in a spaghetti-like nest of tentacles. The ship had grown oddly quiet, no feet along the passageways. Shrugging, Herr Syrup got up, strolled out of the saloon and down a corridor, entered the open main passenger airlock and looked upon the spacefield.

The cigar dropped from his mouth.

The Erse flag was down off the staff and the Anglian banner was back. A long, subdued line of green-clad men shuffled past a heap of their own weapons. Trucks were bringing more every minute. They trailed one by one into a military transport craft berthed nearby, accompanied by hoots and jeers – and an occasional tearful au revoir – from the Grendelian townspeople crowded against the port fence. A troop of redcoats with bayoneted rifles was urging the prisoners along, and the gigantic guns of H.M.S. *Inhospitable* shadowed the entire scene.

'Yudas priest!' said Herr Syrup.

He stumbled down onto the ground. A brisk young officer surveyed him through a monocle, sketched a salute, and extended an arm. 'Mr Syrup? I understand you were aboard. Your crow, sir.'

'Hell and damnation!' said Claus, hopping from the Anglian wrist to the Danish shoulder.

'Pers'nally,' said the young man, 'I go for falcons.'

'You come!' whispered Herr Syrup. 'You come!'

'Just a short hop, don't y' know. We arrived hours back. No resistance, except – er—' The officer blushed. 'I say, don't look now, but that young lady in the, ah, rather brief costume and, er, passionate embrace with the large chappie – d' you know anything about 'em? Mean to say, she claims she's the vicar's daughter and he's her fiancé and she goes where he goes, and really, sir, I jolly well don't know whether to evacuate her with the invaders or give him a permit to remain here or, or what, damn!'

Herr Syrup stole a glance. 'Do vatever seems easiest,' he said. 'I don't t'ink to dem it makes mush difference.'

'No. I suppose not.' The officer sighed.

'How did you find out vat vas happening here? Did de crow really give somevun my message?'

'What message?'

'Go sputz yourself!' rasped Claus.

'No, not dat vun,' said Herr Syrup quickly.

'My dear sir,' said the officer, 'when a half-ruined oxygen bottle, with the name *Mercury Girl* still identifiable on it, lands in a barley field . . . and we've been wirelessed that that ship is under quarantine . . . and then when this black bird flies in a farmer's window and steals a scone off his tea table and says, ah, uncomplimentary things about one Major McConnell . . . well, really, my dear chap, the farmer will phone the police and the police will phone Newer Scotland Yard and the Yard will check with Naval Intelligence and, well, I mean to say it's obvious, eh, what, what, what?'

'*Ja,*' said Herr Syrup weakly. 'I suppose so.' He hesitated. 'Vat you ban going to do vit' de Ersers? Dey vas pretty decent, considering. I vould hate to see dem serving yail sentences.'

'Oh, don't worry about that, sir. Mean to say, well, it's a bally embarrassing situation all around, eh? *We* don't want to admit that a band of half-cocked extremists stole one of our shires right out from under our noses, so to speak, what? We can't suppress the fact, of course, but we aren't exactly anxious to advertise it all over the Solar System, y' know. As for the Erse government, it doesn't want trouble with us – Gaelic Socialists, y' know, peaceful chappies – and certainly doesn't want to give the opposition party a leg up; so they won't support this crazy attempt in any way. At the same time, popular sentiment at home won't let 'em punish the attempt either. Eh?

'Jolly ticklish situation. Delicate. All we can do is ship these fellows home with our compliments, where their own government will doubtless give 'em a talking to and let 'em go. And then, very much on the Q.T., I'm jolly well sure the Erse Republic will pay whatever damage claims there are. Your own ship ought to collect a goodly share of that, eh, what?'

By this time Sarmishkidu von Himmelschmidt had reached the foot of the ladder. 'I'll have you know I have thousands of pounds in damages coming!' he whistled in outrage. 'Maybe millions! Why, just the loss of business during occupation, at a rate of easy five hundred pounds a day – let's call it a t'ousand pounds a day to put it in round figures – dot adds up to—'

'Oh, come now, old chap, come now. Tut-tut!' The officer adjusted his monocle. 'It isn't all that bad. Really it isn't, don't y' know. After all, even if nothing is done officially, word will get around. People will come in jolly old floods to see that place where all this happened. I'll wager my own missus makes me vacation here this season. Cloak and dagger stuff, excitin', all that sort of piffle, eh, what, what? Why, it'll be the busiest tourist season in your history, by Jove.'

'Hmmmm.' Sarmishkidu stroked his nose thoughtfully. A gleam waxed in one bulging eye. 'Hmmm. Yes. The atmosphere of international intrigue; sinister spies, double agents, beautiful females luring away secret papers. Yes, the first place on Grendel to furnish that kind of atmosphere will – Hmmm. I must make some alterations, I see. To hell with *Gemütlichkeit*. I want my tavern to have an uncertain reputation. Yes, that's it, uncertain.' He drew himself up and flourished a dramatic tentacle. 'Gentlemen, you are now looking upon the proprietor of der Alt *Heisenberg* Rathskeller!'

Also in Hamlyn Paperbacks

Robert Silverberg

THE SEED OF EARTH

The computer had chosen them – a small cross-section of humanity to serve Mankind's Destiny. Out of seven billion people on Earth mechanical chance had selected them as involuntary colonists on an unknown planet. In seven days they would be on their way, on a sink-or-swim mission to a lonely world beyond the limits of the Solar System.

It was a summons each had privately dreaded, yet always been prepared for. But no one had prepared them for the vicious attacks of sinister aliens . . .